in violet's wake

D0166808

in violet's wake

{ a novel }

ROBIN DEVEREAUX-NELSON

SOFT SKULL PRESS

This book is a work of fiction. Names, characters, places, and incidents either are products of the author's imagination or are used fictitiously. Any resemblance to actual events or locales or persons, living or dead, is entirely coincidental.

Library of Congress Cataloging-in-Publication Data

Devereaux-Nelson, Robin.
 In Violets Wake : a novel / Robin Devereaux-Nelson.
    pages cm
 ISBN 978-1-59376-534-7 (alk. paper)
 1. Divorced people--Fiction. 2. Male friendship--Fiction. 3. Self-realization--Fiction.
 4. Road fiction. I. Title.
 PS3604.E8855I5 2013
 813'.6--dc23

2013017911

ISBN 978-1-59376-534-7

Cover design by Natalya Bolnova
Interior design by Tabitha Lahr

Soft Skull Press
An Imprint of COUNTERPOINT
1919 Fifth Street
Berkeley, CA 94710
www.softskull.com

Printed in the United States of America
Distributed by Publishers Group West

10 9 8 7 6 5 4 3 2 1

For Jimi
Thanks for getting me. Mostly.

chapter 1

She'd left a half-empty bottle of tequila. She'd left a lot of other things too, but right now Marshall figured the Patrón would serve him better than mismatched dishes, odd socks, and the wedding ring lying in the ceramic dish at the edge of the kitchen sink. Marshall avoided looking at it as he pulled down a glass from the cupboard and poured himself a shot. He waved the tequila under his nose and grimaced. Tequila wasn't his drink; it was Violet's. He turned to the refrigerator and began rummaging in it for a slice of lime or lemon. There was nothing in there but a moldy orange and a net bag with a few withered grapes in it. He left the rotten fruit lying on the refrigerator shelf, scooped up the Patrón, and bravely downed it in a gulp. He poured himself another.

He left the shot glass in the kitchen and took the bottle into the nest he'd built himself in the living room over the last three weeks. The answering machine blinked next to a pile of unopened mail in the foyer. Around him, the house was in shambles—drawers emptied, windows bereft of curtains, all the homey touches packed up and taken away. She'd left behind the things she didn't want, or in Violet-speak, "couldn't bear to take." She'd left those sentimental reminders there for Marshall to deal with, which he did by remaining in a six-by-six-foot area of the living room that included the television, coffee table, and sofa and none of the memorabilia of their short marriage. He stared at the television, seeing nothing, and drank.

When the bottle was empty, Marshall knew what had to be done. Yesterday, he'd found the note shoved into the back of a drawer in the desk, a date and time, Pavlos's name etched in Violet's curlicue handwriting that Marshall'd always thought of as cute. It was stuffed under a photo of her that she'd given him just before she'd moved in. Part of him had wanted to tear it in half, ruin the visage of her dark, smoldering eyes, that half smile that had first attracted him to her, the long, black hair. He used to keep that picture on his nightstand. How long had it been here, in the desk?

Marshall had shoved the photograph back in the drawer, then smoothed the note out on top of the desk. Just looking at the son of a bitch's name made him mad. How long had she been seeing him? And why, after all the things she'd told Marshall about the guy? Pavlos had had his chance with her and blew it. And now, she'd left Marshall for the son of a bitch? It was the only explanation.

Marshall leapt from the sofa, his head reeling, nearly pitching himself onto the floor. He grabbed at the coffee table, upsetting some empty beer cans and an ashtray full of half-smoked cigarettes. He made his way unsteadily to the desk and pulled out the phone book, opening it to the restaurant section. There it was. He jabbed his finger angrily on the page. The Greek's place, Plati Pavlos. Marshall pulled his car keys out of his pants pocket. The fucking guy was going to be sorry.

chapter 2

It was the kind of night Costa Pavlos's mamma used to call a *nychta tou diavolou*—a devil's night. For that matter, things had been off all day. The meat order from Detroit hadn't arrived and he'd had to send Angelina down to the market in town and pay nearly double just to keep them flush for the weekend. Two of the waitresses had gotten into a fight in the ladies room and had to be sent home, and the Hobart had broken down again. He was going to have to spend Sunday afternoon taking the monster mixer apart, and if he couldn't fix it this time, he was going to have to put out a bundle for a new one.

It was a night for dropped glasses, restless patrons, and emotional kitchen staff. So, Costa wasn't surprised when the drunken guy came in around ten and started making a commotion. Marney, the hostess, was doing her best to handle the situation, but the guy towered over her. He was yick-yacking about his wife and waving his keys around. Then, Costa heard the guy start hollering about Costa fooling around with his wife. "What the hell?" the Greek muttered under his breath as he came from behind the bar, hurriedly glancing around the restaurant. That's all Angelina had to hear—he'd be sleeping on the couch for eternity. Thankfully, most of the patrons had already headed out for the night.

"Where's Pavlos!" Marshall was saying. He leaned over the hostess station and knocked the reservation book to the floor. Costa came up behind Marney and put a hand on her shoulder. "Take over the bar, sweetheart." Costa stepped up to Marshall, who was weaving unsteadily on his feet. Up close he reeked of tequila. "What can I do for you, friend?" he asked quietly.

"You Pavlos?"

"Who wants to know?"

Marshall took a lurching step forward. "Violet's husband, that's who!" he hollered, taking a sloppy swing at the older man. Costa caught Marshall's wrist in his meaty hand and jerked him closer. "Sure you want to do that, pal?" Costa said. He chuckled a little, taking in the guy's preppy jacket and loafers. He was tall, all right, but not much heft to him. It was obvious he'd been drinking and that it didn't agree with him. There was a sheen of sweat on the guy's face, which was a bit pale and green.

"You bet!" Marshall said, spraying spittle on Costa's face. Costa twisted Marshall's wrist behind his back, spinning him around. "How 'bout we just sit down and talk about this like gentlemen, huh?" Marshall jerked out of Costa's grip. He swung around fast, waving his long arms to keep his balance, and backed away. Costa shook his head. He walked toward Marshall with his palms out. "Look," he said, "Fella—"

Marshall made a horrible crying sound and rushed forward, head down. He caught Costa in the belly. Costa skidded backward, air coming out of him in an *OOF*, his body shattering the side window. The last table of patrons nervously threw some money down on the bar and scurried toward the door. Marney flattened herself against the liquor rack, and the new dishwasher kid came out of the kitchen, his hands red and wet. "Need help, boss?" he hollered across the room.

Costa pulled himself up and eyed Marshall. Now this skinny guy was pissing him off. He looked at Marshall breathing hard, his excellently cut hair falling in his face. He was holding on to the hostess station to keep his balance. "Nope," Costa said. "I got this." He crooked a finger at Marshall. "That's the way you want it?" he said. "Let's go, sonny boy."

chapter 3

Marshall watched Costa stir tomatoes and onions into the scrambled eggs. The Greek looked up, his face shiny with sweat. "You want some feta, sonny boy?" he said. Marshall nodded. He watched the big man pull a plastic bin of the salty cheese in brine out of the cooler and wondered what Violet had ever seen in this fat fuck.

"Don't call me sonny boy." Marshall took a long swig of his coffee.

"I make you eggs, you godda be an asshole?" The big man slid a spatula under the scrambled eggs and plated them. He topped them off with a fistful of crumbled feta and slid the plate across the counter to Marshall. "Here. Eat. You look like shit." He chuckled. "Sonny boy."

"Fuck you."

Costa put his hands over his heart dramatically. "You're killin' me."

"Really. Whatever, man." Marshall scooped a forkful of eggs into his mouth.

Costa pulled the frying pan from the stove and took it to the big stainless steel sink and ran hot water in it. "How's your head?"

"Not worth a shit." The eggs were good though. Violet used to make him eggs like this. Thinking about it, part of Marshall wanted to puke, knowing the Greek made them for her first. Probably taught her how, right here in this kitchen. He wondered if she'd thought of Pavlos when she made Marshall eggs on Sunday mornings after they'd made love. The bitch.

Christ, he missed her.

Costa pulled a metal stool over to the counter and sat down across from Marshall. "Know what you need?" he said.

"Decapitation?" Marshall rubbed at his sore, red eyes. His head was throbbing.

"Nah," said Costa, producing a bottle of clear liquid from under the counter. "Little hair of the dog." Costa winked at Marshall, opened the bottle of ouzo, and poured a shot in his cup. He slid the bottle across the counter.

Marshall covered his cup with his hand. "No way, man," he said.

"Okay," Costa said, shrugging. Marshall looked the older man over. Considering the night they'd had, Pavlos looked remarkable. His eyes were clear, and he was wearing a clean white T-shirt. He even looked like he'd shaved.

"Oh, what the fuck." Marshall pulled the bottle toward him and poured a shot of the sweet liquor into his coffee. It smelled surprisingly good.

"Your health." Costa raised his cup.

The men clinked their cups together and drank.

"Look," Marshall said, "About last nigh—"

"No worries," Costa replied. "That's why I got insurance." Both men turned to look at the side window. It was covered with heavy cardboard and duct tape. One of the restaurant chairs was lying on a table, three of its legs smashed off.

"Sorry I had to pop you in the face," Costa said. "You godda nice shiner."

"Yeah." Marshall probed his left cheek with a finger and winced. "Hey, I'll fix the window. No use running your premiums up. I was being an asshole."

"We're all assholes." Costa laughed. "Just ask Violet."

Marshall snorted at the mention of Violet's name. "Ain't that the truth."

"Except for Dead Winston," said Costa.

Marshall blinked in recognition. "Oh, yeah. The sainted Dead Winston." He raised his cup. "To Dead Winston." The men drank again.

"He was one lucky son of a bitch," said Costa.

"You got that right."

Marshall stared down into his coffee, thinking about Winston Montgomery. He'd been Violet's first husband, and thirty-two years her senior. They'd met when Violet Benjamin was twenty-two and working one of the many snack bars at Detroit Metro. They'd struck up a conversation over martinis and smoked almonds. He was on his way to Japan to promote one of his company's newest computer programs. She was a college student, still trying to figure out her major. She was bubbly and bright. He was well read and adventuresome.

According to Violet, Win went right out and bullied the girl at the ticket counter, purchased a first-class seat for Violet next to his, and their whirlwind romance began in Tokyo. They came home thirty days later Mr. and Mrs. Winston Montgomery, much to the horror of Marilyn and Tom Benjamin, Violet's parents. Tom referred to him as the Goddamn Cradle Robber until Winston died of a heart attack three years into the marriage. Marilyn never said much about him and secretly nursed a crush on her handsome, distinguished son-in-law so unlike her GM line-working husband.

"Know what I did one time?" Costa said, pulling Marshall out of his reverie. "She used to keep this picture of him on the mantle. Her Poor Dead Winston, she always called him."

"She had a picture of him up in your house while you were married to her?"

"Yeah. Right in the living room so the son of a bitch could watch me watching the Wings game. Used to creep me out. I bitched about it, but she wouldn't get rid of the goddamned thing. Said 'he's my angel watching over me from heaven.' Can you believe that shit? Jealous of a dead guy, that was me, if you can believe that."

Marshall leaned back in his chair. "I can believe it." He hadn't had to endure Winston's photograph, but he'd sure listened to his share of all-the-things-Winston-did-for-me-stories. "So, what'd you do?"

"One night me and Violet were fighting about something." Costa scratched at his head. "Oh, yeah. She went out and bought some clothes and shoes and stuff, and we were kinda hurting for money at the time, you know? Anyhow, I was mad about it. We were standing right there in the living room, and she tells me what a stingy asshole I am being, and we have our own business and whatnot, and how we should be able to afford 'little extravagances,' she called them. Then she says how generous Poor Dead Winston was and blah blah, and she goes stomping to the bedroom and locks herself in." Costa got up from the stool, his knee popping, and crossed to the coffee maker. He filled his cup with steaming black brew. "So, I'm sitting there, right? Having a beer? And I'm looking at the dead guy's picture, smiling at me with all those big white teeth, up there on the fireplace with all these candles and crap, like a goddamned shrine. So I go out the back door and walk over into the neighbor's yard. They have this St. Bernard, right? And he craps all over the fucking place. Everybody in the neighborhood used to bitch about it. So, I go over there and scoop up this big dog turd."

Marshall set his cup down on the stainless counter with a thump. "Jesus! That's disgusting!"

"I scooped it up with a plastic bag. You think I pick up something like that with my hands? Jesus Christ." Costa swirled the coffee around in his cup. "Anyway, I have this gigantic turd, right? And I take it in and put it on the mantle and squash the dead bastard's picture right down in it." Costa sat on the stool and poured another shot of ouzo into his cup. "Laughed my ass off," he said, taking a mouthful of coffee.

"Holy shit."

"Wasn't exactly holy, but it sure was shit!" Costa laughed. "She didn't talk to me for a week."

"Who cleaned up the crap?"

Costa leaned on his forearm and peered over the black plastic frames of his glasses. His licorice breath wafted across the counter. He gave Marshall an incredulous look. "Me. Who do you think cleaned it up?"

Marshall sighed. "Yeah, right."

Costa looked down into his cup. "That one cost me at least two weeks of friggin' therapy."

"You, too, huh?"

Costa nodded. "She was always going to some shrink or other.

Cost us a mint." He gestured around the room. "You got your own business, you gotta pay your own insurance premiums, take care of your property."

"I hear that," Marshall said. "Started my own office about a year and a half ago."

"Yeah?" Costa said. He patted Marshall's shoulder. "Good for you. So, what happened?"

"What do you mean, what happened?"

"Between the two of you. You and Violet."

"I don't know for sure." Marshall rubbed his throbbing head. "She said I was unhappy. I guess I wasn't ecstatic about how things were between us, but all couples go through stuff, you know? I didn't think things were bad. I mean, hell. We weren't talking as much as we used to, and certainly things changed—you know, in the bedroom. But it wasn't bad, you know? Shit, my mom and dad—hell, they'd fight like crazy. My mom would be screaming, and she'd take her shoes off and throw them at my dad."

"She Greek?"

"French and Polish." Marshall hunched over his coffee, his voice going quiet. "But, you know, for all their fighting, they stayed together. My mom totally lost it when my dad died, said he was the love of her life." He chuckled softly. "All us kids could remember was yelling and flying shoes. But me and Violet? Things weren't bad enough for . . . this." Costa nodded. "Maybe she'll change her mind," Marshall said. "Come back, you know. Maybe she's just . . . wanting some . . . space. Or something." Marshall thought about Violet's wedding ring, lying in a little dish next to the kitchen sink at home.

"Sure, maybe she'll, you know, come back," said Costa, but he looked down into his coffee when he said it, and Marshall could tell he didn't think that was going to happen.

chapter 4

Costa locked the restaurant door behind Marshall with a sigh, shaking his head. He ran a hand through his thick hair. He had to admit, he felt sorry for the guy. After all, he'd been there. Costa had been Violet's second husband. He was first generation American, the son of Greek immigrants, and grew up in his father's restaurant in Detroit. Violet hadn't liked Detroit, and she was even less fond of Costa's conventional mother, Marta, who never let Costa forget he hadn't married a Greek. Thin, pale Violet was a slap in his mother's face, and when it got out that Violet couldn't have children, his traditional mother was relentless. Every time she saw Violet she screamed obscenities, cried, and locked herself in the restaurant basement refusing to come upstairs until "that barren white whore" had left the premises.

For the sake of his own sanity, Costa's father decided he needed to expand the business, and he set Costa up in Saginaw with a new restaurant. When Costa added a nightclub to the restaurant, his father was livid. Told him it would only bring trouble. Good thing he'd never told his father the club was Violet's idea. She'd hated the restaurant and refused to work there alongside her husband the way Marta had worked alongside his father all their lives. But a club, she said, that could be her baby. She would be the manager and hostess. Unfortunately, what that really meant was Violet partying and flirting every night with the regulars. Costa was jealous, and they fought constantly, made up passionately. Emotionally speaking, they were always in high gear.

It was the childlessness, however, that broke the camel's back for the couple. Costa's cousin Niki and his wife came up from Detroit to help with the Saginaw enterprise, which was booming. The couple had a little girl, Eva. She was a gorgeous two-year-old with rosy skin and black hair, little wet brown eyes that flashed. Costa was enchanted.

Costa loved sharing their home with them—he'd missed having family around. His parents had never visited, always saying they were too busy with the Detroit business, but Costa knew it was because of Violet. He wished they could see in her what he saw—a woman who was beautiful, smart, vibrant. Violet ate up life like it was a baklava, full of sweet nuttiness, rich butter, and honey.

Violet, though outwardly congenial, soon resented the camaraderie of Costa, Niki, and his pretty wife, Olivia. She complained about their late-night drinking and laughter. She disliked having another woman in her kitchen, even though Costa teasingly told Violet she was not the most domestic woman in the world, so why did she care about the kitchen now?

But it was Eva of whom Violet was most jealous. The girl had Costa wrapped around her little finger. He would sneak home after the lunch rush, send the sitter out, and sit rocking the little girl to sleep for her nap, singing lullabies in Greek. He spoiled her with gifts, told her she was beautiful, sweet, smart—all of the things he used to say to Violet.

One night as he was reading the little girl a bedtime story, he heard a rustling in the hallway. He laid Eva in her crib and softly walked to the guest-room door, surprising a tearful Violet. She was wearing her coat and gloves, two large suitcases at her feet.

"What are you doing?" Costa asked her.

"I can't stand it anymore."

"Stand? Stand what?" He put his hands on her shoulders, but she shrugged him away. "Violet. I'm sorry. I'll tell Niki he has to find a place. This week. I promise."

"No, Costa," she said. "I don't care about that." Tears streamed down her ivory cheeks. She looked tragically beautiful, heartbreaking. "It's her." She inclined her head toward the doorway of the guest room.

"Eva?" Costa was incredulous. "Violet, grow up. She's a little baby."

"She's what I can't give you," Violet said. "Ever." She picked up her bags. "I love you, Costa. But I have to go."

At first, Costa hadn't worried. Violet had left many times before, and after several passionate phone calls between the couple, she had come back. Each time it was like having a honeymoon all over again. It had gotten to a point that Costa almost looked forward to these little forays of hers. Really spiced things up. "Nothing like a little hot blood," his father used to say.

But this time she really disappeared. He tried all her regular haunts. Her family'd never approved of him, so they would barely speak to him. Even the cops had been little help. Wives and husbands left their spouses all the time. To the cops, he was just some poor schmuck who'd gotten dumped. They'd reluctantly filed a missing person's report, but it had brought no news. He had to face the fact that Violet didn't want to be found. Costa was beside himself with worry and remorse, in complete despair. And then, three months after the day she left, divorce papers arrived in the mail from some little town up North. Next thing he heard, Violet was marrying some Hicksville guy.

Remembering what happened brought it all back. Violet had said she loved him when she left. Costa had been sure she'd come back—just like that poor sap, Marshall. Costa recalled it had been especially lonely when Niki, Olivia, and Eva left for their new house in the suburbs. He hadn't even told his parents Violet had left him, and he threatened Niki with death if he revealed the truth. He didn't want to suffer the I-told-you-so, the shame, his mother's gloating laughter. Marshall was on his own. Costa knew the guy had a long road ahead of him.

After Violet left Costa, he'd had his own long road—in fact, he'd almost lost the restaurant, disappearing into drink, sitting in his house in the dark, in the bedroom he'd shared with Violet. If it hadn't been for Niki, he would have lost everything. He owed his cousin his living. And more. But then, that's what family was for, right? Violet had never really understood that.

He remembered his despair, the way he wanted to hunt her and her new lover down, the way her behavior in the club played over and over in his head. Pictures of Violet laughing, dancing, letting men buy her drinks. "Don't be jealous," she'd said. "I'm just being friendly—and they're buying your liquor and food, tipping the girls. Don't be a baby," she'd said. A baby. He was no baby. He was a man.

But he remembered feeling like a baby, when he knew she was gone for good. How he'd lain in their bed, drunk and stupid, crying big man tears into the pillow. Trashing his own restaurant. It'd cost him a bundle to repair his own destruction.

He thought again about Marshall and how he'd broken the window and they'd smashed up the restaurant. Marshall was as messed up as Costa had been back then.

DATE: 09-22-2011

CLIENT: Violet Mary VanDahmm nee. Benjamin

CASE NUMBER: V2011-100982

DATE OF BIRTH: 09-17-1972

PRESENTING PROBLEM:

Violet is an intelligent separated thirty-nine-year-old white woman who is self-referred to this practice. She states that she recently acquired a job as an executive's assistant at a real estate company but also states she does not like the position. Violet is seeking therapy because she is recently separated from her sixth husband, Marshall. She states she is not sleeping well and has been feeling anxious in general "for a long time." She states she has benefited from talk therapy in the past and wishes to work on, in her words, "identity and abandonment" issues. When asked why she did not return to her former therapist, Violet stated that he did not understand her. She refused to discuss this further.

HISTORY:

Prior to the initial intake appointment, Violet signed a waiver releasing her past therapy records to this office. Patient notes from a Dr. Eric Coulter have been received and reviewed, as well as several group therapy notes from the Center for Awakening. Violet was born in Saginaw, Michigan, to working-class parents. She is an only child. She has had significant issues with her mother and her uninvolved, yet present, father. She reported being an awkward, overweight teenager with few friends. Patient notes state Violet was "moody" and taken to bouts of self-centered dreaminess, and was an average, unmotivated student whose greatest interest was theatre and art.

She first sought therapy while married to her first husband, Winston Montgomery, to "work out childhood issues." The first husband was an affluent entrepreneur some years her senior. He died three years into the marriage. Violet continued therapy with Dr. Coulter into the second marriage to a restaurateur, Costa Pavlos, until Mr. Pavlos refused to pay for continued therapy, after which Violet attended several group therapy sessions at the Center for Awakening, a new age, self-exploration counseling endeavor.

MEDICAL PROBLEMS:
Nothing significant noted.

CURRENT PRECSRIPTION MEDICATIONS:
Client states she has previously taken Xanax and Ambien on an as-needed basis, but that her prescription has lapsed.

MOOD AND AFFECT:
At first impression, Violet presents as slightly narcissistic, with a need for admiration and inflated self-involvement. There is a sense of a lack of empathy when discussing past relationships (with her six husbands) and parents, whom, she states, "never understood" her. However, there is a sweetness and genuineness about her that is charming, and her lack of empathy does not

come off as either cruel or deliberate. She is attractive and carefully (albeit somewhat seductively) dressed, articulate, and seems to be quite intelligent.

SESSION NOTES:

Violet and I went over past case notes and talked briefly about her recent separation from her sixth husband, who she describes as sweet but distant and unhappy. She says her decision to leave him is "difficult" but "necessary" due to her "emotional and spiritual growth" and "realizations" about herself and her needs. Our time concluded at this juncture.

TREATMENT RECOMMENDATIONS:

Therapy sessions will be set for twice per month, unless circumstances require more (or less) time. Violet has been referred to her medical doctor for prescriptions of anti-anxiety medication and to make a recommendation of whether any other medications are needed to assist her with sleeplessness.

Yolanda H. Malik, LCSW
Champoor and Associates

chapter 5

Marshall's cell phone rang at 8:00 AM on Sunday morning, jarring him out of a hard sleep. Truth was, he'd slept most of Saturday, nursing his raging hangover. Thank God he'd picked a Friday night to be an asshole. Gave him the weekend to get straight. He pulled the phone off the coffee table and looked at the caller ID. He didn't recognize the number, so he let it go to voicemail and settled back on the sofa, where he'd been sleeping since Violet had left. He just couldn't bring himself to lie in the bed they'd shared.

The phone went off again. Marshall snatched it up and flipped it open.

"What?" he barked.

"Sonny boy, it's Costa."

Marshall ran a hand through his hair. "Jesus, do you know what time it is? What the hell do you want?"

"I let you sleep in my place and feed you and drink with you and you godda be an asshole?"

Marshall swung his legs off the sofa and sat up, disliking the slightly dizzy feeling in his head. "Okay, man," he said, taking a deep breath. "What's up? Is that better?"

"Sure."

"So, what do you want?"

"I have something you godda see."

Marshall looked at the mess around him, at his wrinkled clothes, the empties on the coffee table. "I'm . . . busy."

"Right." Marshall heard Costa take a slurp of something. "Look," the man continued, "I lied to Angelina about why I'm not at church, so don't bullshit a bullshitter, all right?" Marshall sighed. "I know what you're going through," Costa continued. "So, put your fucking coat on and come outside. I'm sitting in your driveway."

Marshall was off the sofa like a shot. He pulled the front door open. "What the fuck, man?" he said into the phone. Costa was looking at him through the windshield of his Ford Ranger.

"I told you. I'm in your driveway."

Marshall sputtered. "How did you know where I lived, you fat fuck?"

Marshall stood shuddering on the front stoop in his stocking feet, glaring at Costa through the windshield. He watched the big man reach down on the seat, then hold up a small rectangle-shaped object so Marshall could see it.

"Where's your wallet, huh, sonny boy?" Costa was grinning.

"Son of a bitch," Marshall muttered.

"You're gonna freeze," Costa said. "Now, go put on your goddamned coat and shoes and go for a ride with me."

"Whatever," Marshall mumbled. He turned to go in.

"And, sonny boy?" Costa said into the phone. Marshall turned back and looked at the older man from the doorway. "Comb your hair. You look like shit."

When Marshall climbed in the truck a few minutes later, Costa handed him a Styrofoam container of coffee. "Cream. Sugar," he said.

"How'd you know?"

"You look like cream and sugar."

"What the fuck does that mean?"

Costa chuckled. "Don't get your underpants in a twist, sonny boy. Wasn't an insult. I been workin' in the restaurant business since I was old enough to hold my own dick over the edge of the pot. You get to learn what people are gonna order, how they like things."

"Really." Marshall's head throbbed, and the smell of the coffee wafting from the container was inviting.

"Do you like cream and sugar in your coffee, sonny boy?"

"Yeah," Marshall mumbled. He popped the lid off the cup and took a long drink of the coffee, which, he had to admit, was prepared just the way he liked it. Costa tossed a white, waxed bag in his lap.

"Doughnut?"

Marshall made a move to open the bag, then stopped, looking intently at Costa. "Don't tell me," he said.

"Sour cream with cinnamon and sugar." They said it at the same time. Costa grinned.

"How do you do that?"

Costa shrugged, turning the key in the ignition and throwing the truck into gear. "Don't know. My pop used to do it too." The big man pulled onto the street and headed north.

"Where the hell we going?" Marshall bit into the doughnut, sugar and cinnamon spilling onto his jacket. He brushed it away.

"Omer," said Costa.

"Omer? What the hell is that?"

"Little town on 23," said Costa. "We're going to see Hubcap."

"Hubcap?"

"Brian Jankowicz. He was Violet's third husband. After me. The locals call him Hubcap."

"Do I want to know why?"

Costa began to chuckle again. "Oh, sonny boy, you'll see."

Marshall popped the last of the doughnut in his mouth and washed it down with the coffee. He watched the neighborhood slide by. "Look," said Marshall, "can you stop calling me that?"

"Okay," Costa said, his grin wide and white. "Sonny boy."

chapter 6

When Brian Jankowicz met Violet Benjamin-Montgomery-Pavlos in Beanies, a little bar on the Au Sable River on a rainy April night, the thing he noticed was that she looked totally out of place. Girls that walked into Beanies generally wore tight jeans and tighter T-shirts, tennis shoes or boots, and hairdos straight out of 1985. Violet sat shivering at the end of the bar, nursing a cup of Beanie's nasty coffee, wearing a wrap-around knit dress and low heels. She had a hat on, which Brian thought looked pretty classy. It was one of those wool hats, like a man's, but it was a pearly gray color and had a paisley hatband. Her dark hair was damp, her fingers raw and red.

The other thing that struck Brian as strange was how the woman had gotten there. He knew everyone's car in Omer—he was the only mechanic in the small village—and the only cars in the parking lot were Jessa's, the bartender, and old man Weaver's 1962 Chevy pickup. Brian figured right quick the woman must have had some car trouble. And from the looks of her, other trouble as well. He'd seen that same sad look on his own mother's face plenty of times. Definitely some man problems.

Brian sidled up to the bar, and Jessa slid him a draught of Miller. He tipped his head at her and laid two dollars on the bar. As he sat down, he caught the woman's eye and nodded to her.

"How ya' doin'?" he said.

"I've been better," said Violet, glancing around nervously.

"Had some car trouble, did you?" Brian took a drink of his beer. She sat back in her chair, her eyes going wide with alarm. "How did you know that?" she demanded.

"Parking lot," Brian explained. "Only two cars." He nodded toward Jessa and Inky Weaver.

"Oh." Violet's huge doe-eyes caught Brian's green ones and nailed him to his seat. Something in his stomach did a flip-flop. It was not an entirely unpleasant sensation. She was so petite and pretty. Brian caught himself staring.

"Have you called anyone?" he asked. It came out all hoarse and squeaky. He cleared his throat nervously, and Jessa looked over at him and snickered. He shot her a dirty look.

Violet's eyes welled. "I . . . I just left my husband," she said, blinking rapidly to quell the tears.

Brian slid over in the seat next to her. He grabbed a handful of napkins from a stack on the bar and handed them to Violet. "Oh, hey," he said. "I'm sorry."

"Thank you." Violet took the napkins and wiped at her eyes. "I was just upset, you know? And I guess I wasn't paying enough attention. To where I was going or the car."

"Understandable," Brian pushed his dark blonde hair out of his eyes. He wished he'd gotten that haircut last week like he'd intended. He was glad he'd gone home and showered off the greasy dirt of the garage before coming down for a beer. He smoothed his flannel shirt and gave himself a cursory glance in the mirror behind the bar. "I know what it's like."

"You're divorced?"

"Oh . . . um . . . no," Brian stammered. "There was this girl though . . . it was really, you know, tough when we split." Another snicker from Jessa. Brian narrowed his eyes at her, and she turned from the couple and made a show of wiping at some bar glasses.

"Yes," Violet said, blowing her nose on a bar napkin "It's . . . difficult."

"Listen, where's your car?" Brian asked. "Maybe I can help?" Violet told him she'd made a wrong turn off US 23 about a mile down the road. She'd walked back to Beanies after the car went dead.

"You walked on a dirt road in those shoes?" Brian said, grinning.

This got a wan smile out of Violet. "Yeah. Not too smart, huh." She wiped at her eyes again. "I mean, I had tennis shoes in the car. I just didn't feel like digging through all the stuff in the back for my bag in the rain and all."

Brian told her he was a mechanic and offered to get her car running. He'd thrown a tenner at Jessa and told her to make Violet something hot to eat, then promised Inky he'd buy him a couple of beers if he drove Brian out to round up Violet's car. "And I'll bring your bag back too, if you want." Brian offered. "So you can put something warm and dry on."

✳ ✳ ✳

That evening, Brian introduced Violet to his Aunt Linda who owned a rooming house in the village, and before long she and Brian started seeing each other, much to Aunt Linda's displeasure. There was something about that girl she hadn't liked. She was too . . . perfect, which Linda translated as phony.

For Violet though, Omer turned out to be a great place to hide out. She was a tragic princess, and Brian enjoyed playing the hero. She told him about her life with Costa, how she couldn't give him a child, about what hard work it was, owning the restaurant and club. How she just wasn't appreciated by the Pavlos family. Brian listened to Violet's stories, held her hand, told her she was wonderful and what a shame it was that other people just couldn't see that. She listened to him, too—and he shyly found his way to telling her things he'd never talked about before. He'd look at himself in the mirror, seeing his long, skinny frame, his pale skin, and his longish curly hair that just never seemed to look right, and he'd wonder how he'd gotten so lucky. It was just like an angel had fallen right out of the sky.

When Violet's divorce from Costa Pavlos was final, Brian asked her to marry him. He was scared to death that she'd say no, but she just jumped into his lap and put her arms around his neck and cried that he was the sweetest thing. They bought a little ranch-style house on an acre of land bordered by fields and a wooded lot. Violet lay in Brian's arms at night filling him in on her childhood and her abandonment issues, her life with Poor Dead Winston, with Costa, about therapy and the support groups that she found to be so comforting. It was then that Brian revealed his issue as well: He was bipolar—but on his medication. And thanks to Violet coming into his life, he would stay on it this time.

This promise made Brian's sisters, mother, and Aunt Linda roll their eyes. How many times had they heard that? They weren't crazy about Violet either. She was stuck up, they said. Thought she was better than everybody else. Wanting to drink wine with funny names rather than have a cold beer. Not going to bingo with the other women. Reading, for Christ's sake. Painting the rooms in the house funny colors. Who could understand it?

Violet wept and told Brian how this always happened to her, how she was continually ostracized. It had happened with the Pavlos family, the Montgomerys—with her own parents, for that matter, the girls at school. She'd cry big, fat tears, and tender-hearted Brian would find his eyes welling, too, as he took her in his arms. Did he think they were . . . jealous of her, she wanted to know? Brian didn't know about that, but what he did know was that his position between the bickering women in his family made him more than a little uncomfortable—in fact, it felt down-right dangerous at times, and he'd had many a heated argument trying to get them to include Violet.

So Violet learned to play bingo and went to Beanies on Friday nights with Brian to shoot pool, and the women grudgingly made an attempt to include her. She tried gardening with Aunt Linda but was a miserable failure at it. She was bored, and Brian's mechanic's paycheck was far below anything Violet was used to. She'd even gone into Standish and tried to find a job herself, but it was hopeless unless she wanted to waitress, which, of course, she did not. No way.

They fought about it. Brian wanted her to contribute—his salary as a mechanic was meager, even though he worked hard and steadily. Violet told him she'd been to college and she'd taken a few business classes—she could do better than restaurant work. She'd never even waited tables when she was with Costa and they owned the restaurant, so why would she want to do that now? She wanted to work in an office, but with no secretarial experience, there was nothing available. By the time Brian was sorry about the arguments, it was far too late. Violet was unhappy.

Then she began to say things that made him feel confused. Things like she could see how unhappy *he* was, how she could see she wasn't the right one for *him*. That no matter how hard she tried, his family would never accept her, and she couldn't bear to see him torn between them and her. That he'd be better off without her. No matter how much he protested and told her how much he loved her, she walked around with a sad little smile. He began to drink a little more than usual. Not long after that, he started forgetting to take his medication.

It was a quick spiral downward. Despite Violet's many years of therapy and group work, she had no idea what to do when presented with an actual mental health situation. Brian knew his bouts of euphoria were more palatable to her—the times when he felt sublimely, wanting to dance in the grass with her barefoot in the early morning dew. But when the blackness came upon him, Brian could see that Violet was terrified.

One night, Brian staggered into Beanies talking crazy. His shaggy hair was dirty and unkempt, and though it was freezing outside, he wore no jacket. He kept saying someone had drugged him, kept slurring his words, his eyes rolling alarmingly up into his head. Violet called the bar looking for him, but instead of calling his wife, Jessa had already phoned Brian's mother, who said she'd be right over. She'd seen Brian like this many times before.

The ambulance arrived just seconds before Violet did. She watched Mrs. Jankowicz take charge with the EMTs, ignoring Violet's presence, giving them the list of Brian's medications, his history, getting him packed into the ambulance. As it pulled out of the driveway, Brian's mother looked at Violet. "Well, come on," she said tersely, pulling her windbreaker around her, her cigarette clamped between her yellow teeth.

"I . . . uh . . . I'll drive in my car," Violet said weakly.

"Suit yourself," Mrs. Jankowicz said, walking away from Violet. Then under her breath, "You stupid little bitch."

Violet never showed up at the hospital. A month later, Brian received divorce papers from an attorney in Bay City. He was despondent, spending long hours sifting through the junk in the back of the garage, refusing the work folks brought to him. After finding the beginnings of an old hubcap collection his dad had started years ago, Brian took an unnatural interest in it. He began visiting the junkyard, collecting, stacking, piling, and matching the wheel covers inside his house. When his mom wouldn't stop bitching about it, he began nailing them to his house. It started innocently enough, like any obsession.

chapter 7

Costa and Marshall came upon their destination around 10:00 AM. Omer was one of those small Michigan towns you'd miss if you blinked, other than the road signs which proudly announced that the village was the Sucker Capitol of the World.

"Are you fucking kidding me?" Marshall said. "Sucker Capitol?"

"It's a fish," said Costa.

"A sucker fish?"

"Not sucker *fish*, just sucker. It's a bottom feeder."

"Whatever," said Marshall, laughing.

The men drove through the small village, which took all of ten seconds. About two miles further north, Costa pulled off 23 onto a lumpy dirt road. Marshall looked around at the naked trees, the yards with sad little ranch-style or farm homes sitting in yards sporting hulking, junked-out cars and piles of old tires. Everything was dull, gray, and soggy brown. Even the sky was a dirty yellowish blanket. Marshall hated fall. It was a season of dying.

"How much farther?" he said to Costa.

"Just up the road a ways."

Marshall peered out the window at the gloomy trees. Through the branches and trunks the wan sun winked off a surface that looked to Marshall like some type of body of water.

"What's out there? A pond or something?"

"You'll see. That's what I wanted to show you."

"Okay, Costa. I've seen ponds before. Lakes. Rivers. Jesus, I've even seen the fucking ocean. We're in Michigan, man. Water wonderland. What's the big mystery?"

"Isn't water," said Costa. The truck bumped over the dirt road. "Look." He pointed between the trees.

Marshall pulled off his Ray Bans and leaned, squinting over the dashboard. "What *is* that? Looks like some kind of fucking spaceship or something." Costa just chuckled and pulled the truck up a little further along the dirt road. Marshall rolled the window down and stuck his head out, trying to get a better view. There was a silvery flickering back beyond the copse of oak, scrub pines, and poplar. In a clearing beyond the trees, Marshall could now see a small ranch-style house. It was covered from roof to ground with shiny, silver hubcaps. The dull autumn sun reflected points of light off the chrome, making the house look like some sort of surreal oracle set in the midst of the wooded lot.

"Holy shit," Marshall said, leaning out to get a better look. Costa pulled the truck over to the side of the road. He drained his coffee, squashing the empty cup in his hand and whipping it onto the floor, which was covered with similar trash.

"Hubcap's house," said Costa.

"Pull up a little further," Marshall said, still staring out the windshield. "That is the most fucking bizarre thing I've ever fucking seen."

"No shit. That's why I had to show you. And we are close enough, my friend."

"Wait," said Marshall, sitting back on the seat and regarding Costa. "You had to show me this, why exactly?"

"You want to end up like that? Bat shit crazy living in a house covered in hubcaps?"

Marshall laughed, but it didn't sound very convincing. "You're fucked up, man."

"No, my friend, you're fucked up."

Marshall stared out the window. He thought about the little six-by-six cave he'd created for himself at home, the drinking, the fact that he hadn't shown up at his own office for nearly two weeks.

"What'd you come in my restaurant for? Huh?" Costa had turned in his seat and was looking intently at Marshall.

"I don't know . . . I . . ." He looked away. He fidgeted with his hands in his lap. Then he growled, "What do people usually come into a restaurant for?"

"You came in there looking for me. Wanted to see what kind of a fuckup I was, so you could figure out what kind of fuckup you are." Marshall was silent. Costa pointed a finger at him. "Lemme ask you this—how many days you call in sick to work this week?"

"Fuck you."

Costa put his hand on the younger man's shoulder. "I almost lost everything after Violet," he said. "It tore me up to lose her." He sat back and laughed. "I know she's a crazy broad. But you know what? Sometimes I still miss things about her." Costa's eyes got a faraway look. He smiled a little, but it was a sad smile. "Yeah, Angelina would fucking kill me if she knew that." Costa reached in his pocket and pulled out a coin, rubbing at it thoughtfully with his thumb. "Know what I missed most?"

"What?" Marshall sat staring out the window at the chrome-covered house of Brian Jankowicz.

"The way she smelled in the morning. Not a perfume. I can't explain it. It was—"

"*Her* smell," Marshall finished. He swallowed hard.

"Yeah," said Costa. "And the way her hair was this big net of black fuzz and her eyes were almost Chinese-looking." Costa sighed. "She looked like a little cat to me then. Sweet, you know?"

Marshall nodded. The men sat looking at the winking, metal-covered house. "So, what happened to him?" Marshall said.

"I don't know for sure," Costa said. "He went crazy, I guess." He pulled a pack of gum absently out of his shirt pocket, glommed two sticks, and handed one to Marshall. The truck filled with the sweet minty scent.

Marshall chewed, lost in thought. Without taking his eyes from Jankowicz's property, he said to Costa, "Let's go ask him."

"What the fuck you talkin' about?"

"Let's go talk to him," said Marshall, a bit more insistent. Costa was waving his hands at Marshall, shaking his head.

"No way. What would we say? We were here spying on your crazy ass and we just thought we'd drop in and say hi?"

"We'll tell him we're starting a support group," said Marshall. "Just like those crazy fucking groups Violet was always going to."

"Jesus, you got that right. Cost me a bundle. I don't do no crazy support group shit. Let's go." He put his hand on the ignition.

"Oh, really?" Marshall said. "Why was it again you came to pick me up today?"

Costa sighed and dropped his hand back in his lap. "Oh, come on. I saw how you were Friday night. You didn't mean to bust up my place. You're just messed up right now."

"Right," said Marshall. "You wanted to . . . help me get through it."

"Okay," said Costa, throwing his hands up into the air. "Whatever."

"And think about it, Costa! How many of us are there?"

"Us?"

"Ex-husbands. Of Violet's."

"Hmmm." Costa rubbed his wide forehead. "Well, me, you, Hubcap," he said, counting on this fingers.

"Dead Winston," they said at the same time.

"Then between Hubcap and you . . . I can't remember," said Costa.

"There was that guy from Indiana. Tim something," Marshall said.

"Oh yeah. And who was that other guy? The veterinarian?"

"Oh, shit, yeah! Owen. How come you know about all these guys? They were after you and Violet. You keep track?"

Costa's face turned red and he looked out his window at nothing in particular. "Maybe," he said.

"Why?"

"Who knows . . . Maybe I am one of those whadayacallits . . . masochists. Anyhow, I heard that this Brian guy went off the deep end and covered the house in hubcaps. Had to see it for myself, so one Sunday I take a ride out here. And what the fuck? It's true. So, now you see it for yourself. Crazy. You wanna end up like that?"

"Let's go talk to him," Marshall said again. Costa sat, silent. "Hey, it's your fault. You brought me out here."

"I don't wanna talk to no nut." Costa fidgeted with his keys.

"But you want to *spy* on a nut? Nice."

After another moment of silence, Costa looked over at Marshall. "Not very polite to show up empty-handed," he said.

"True enough," said Marshall. "Let's go back into Omer and pick up some beers."

chapter 8

Owen Blanton was the most affluent veterinarian in his town. His practice was housed in a sprawling brick hacienda on a wooded acre of Mackinaw Road. It was Sunday, but he was sitting in his office, finishing notes on the emergency surgery he'd had to perform that morning on the Johnstone's Siamese. He was looking out the window at the dry brown leaves that remained on the trees at the edge of the lot when Violet called to say she wanted to get together. "I've left Marshall," she said. Of all the ex-husbands, Owen was the only one who'd stayed in touch with her. They'd worked out a "friendly divorce." More accurately, Owen hid his true feelings for the sake of avoiding confrontation. She hadn't wanted the house, or his business, just some money. So, they'd worked it out.

"Seriously?" Owen said, holding the phone in the crook between his neck and shoulder. He pushed the scattered files into a messy pile and moved the stack back into his "IN" basket. He'd have to tackle them another day. "I thought Marshall was *the one.*"

"So did I," said Violet. She was beginning to get that pout in her voice that grated on Owen's nerves, so he decided it was easier to tell her he'd meet her instead of trying to get out if it. Just when he'd promised himself he was going to try to keep his distance, too. They agreed on lunch at Hoffbecks because it was close to his office and because they both knew how much Owen liked the Caesar salad there. Violet always was one to subtly woo. Especially when she wanted something.

She was sitting at their usual table when Owen walked in. It threw him sometimes, when she did things like that, like she had when they were married. Sitting at *their* table. It was like the divorce never happened, like she was meeting him for lunch like always. Owen remembered when they were first married, the many times they hadn't even made it through their lunch, rushing instead back to the clinic to make love on the leather sofa in his office with the sounds of dogs barking through the walls and the musky smell of fur and medicine all around them. Those were good times.

Her jet-black hair was shorter, cut into a fashionable bob that framed her face and made her eyes look even larger. In Owen's book, they were her best feature, rimmed with long, black lashes. Dark brown with tiny flecks of gold, if you looked close enough. And Owen always did. Her clingy knit top showed off her small waist and great breasts—there was something to be said for never having had a child. Violet had the body of a twenty-year-old even though she was just turning forty. She had those skinny jeans on, the ones that hugged her calves and thighs, and she was wearing kitchy leather boots that looked old, like they were from the '60s.

Owen took her all in. He didn't want to admit it to himself, but every time they got together, for a drink, lunch—even though she was remarried—he always had a smidgen of hope. When

they'd divorced, Violet almost immediately slid into a relationship, then marriage, with Tim Stark, and Owen had been livid,
hurt. He'd spent a couple years trying to pretend, with no suc-
cess, that Violet didn't exist, that their marriage hadn't, in fact.
Then one day he ran into her on the street, and he realized he
still missed her. She'd told him things were not good between
Tim and her, and they'd agreed to meet for a drink. Little by little,
they'd formed a friendship, though Owen hoped for more.

Now, despite her quirks and downright irritating traits, he
still felt warm whenever he was around her. Being her pal allowed
him to stay near. So, he was her pal. She'd even invited him to
the wedding when she married Marshall VanDahmm, but he'd
begged off. Said he had to be at a veterinary convention in Columbus. Though he knew about her growing relationship with
Marshall, he'd still held out hope. Watching her marry someone
else? There was only so much a guy could take.

Violet greeted him warmly, as usual, getting up from the
table to bestow a platonic hug. Her hair brushed his face, and
he breathed it in—her smell. He still missed that. It'd been seven
years since the divorce, and though he'd dated a little—at Violet's
urging, in fact—nothing had panned out. He'd even adopted an
abandoned mutt one of his clients had found by the side of the
road, despite years of petlessness.

That had been one of the things he'd loved about Violet. She
hadn't wanted pets in the house. Most people assumed veterinar-
ians had menageries of animals at home, but after ten-hour days
of sticking your fingers in animal orifices, you really didn't want
to deal with that when you got home. Owen had wondered more
than once about the sex lives of gynecologists.

"Thanks for meeting me." Violet had that look about her that
she got when she was working up a good cry. Owen knew she

was a drama queen, but he'd never really minded much. She was animated and essentially sweet, and back when they were married, after a day of dealing with animals, her dramatic stories of what happened during her day, what her mother had the nerve to say to her when she called, maybe she should enroll in some classes and "expand her mind," (and decrease Owen's bank account, he always thought, but never said aloud), and reminiscing about some childhood slight eased Owen. It was like having your gramma read you a scary bedtime story in a sweet, soothing voice.

Now, instead of a wife, he came home to Bentley jumping and slobbering on him, Bentley who loved him unconditionally no matter how much Owen ignored him. Bentley was no replacement for Violet, but it helped not having to come home to an empty house. And Owen had to admit, the furry beast was growing on him.

"How are you?" Violet had that knack, always asking about you first, then launching into a self-centered dissertation of what was going on with her. It threw you, until you understood what she was up to. Owen had no illusions. He was much like Bentley. Unconditional.

"No, how are you?" Owen said, patting her arm. "You called me, remember?" Violet's eyes got misty. She took a preparatory tissue out of her handbag. Owen steeled himself. Why did he have to be such a softie? "So," he said, "what's happened between you and Marshall?"

"Oh, Owen!" Violet said, and she began to sniffle. She wiped at her carefully made-up eyes. Couldn't have the eyeliner smudged, oh, no.

"Things haven't been good between me and Marshall for a while," she said with a dramatic sigh.

"Um, hmmm . . ." Owen nodded in what he hoped was an encouraging manner. He was thinking, *I wonder if Marshall knows that.*

Violet went on to tell him how they'd been struggling for money and yet she felt Marshall didn't want her to work—it would make him feel like less of a man, poor guy, with his issues with his dad and all.

"Well, what would you do?" Owen asked, knowing full well Violet had little practical experience in the working world.

"Oh, I don't know." Violet wiped at her eyes again. "I hate working at the real estate office. I was thinking about getting my paralegal certification, you know, work in an attorney's office or something." She leaned forward and lowered her voice. "Before I got this job, I went over to see Costa. To see if he'd let me re-open the club."

"You're kidding," Owen said. "I thought you told me he was abusive to you. And that the club was a money pit."

Violet fluttered her eyelashes. "Well, not exactly *abusive*. Just mentally maybe . . . and more his family than him. He's really just a big old bear, you know. A softie inside."

Owen thought about the many tearful revelations she'd shared about Costa over the years, the therapy bills he himself had paid to help her "work through the abuse." Jesus Christ. "So," he said noncommittally. "What'd he say?"

"He shooed me out. Angelina was there." Violet leaned forward, giving Owen a more than healthy view of her cleavage. Owen blinked and leaned forward. He nervously cleared his throat. "You know how jealous she is of me. He said, 'Are you fugging kidding me, Violet? Angie would have my balls.'" Violet stuffed the used tissue back in her bag and sighed. "So, that was that."

"I don't think Marshall would have been crazy about you working for your ex-husband," Owen said, thinking, *I would have never put up with her working for that slob.* "You know," he leaned over and covered Violet's hand with his own, "I wouldn't have minded that. Trust wasn't an issue between us, Violet."

"Oh, Owen. You're sweet," she said, brushing her fingers across his knuckles, giving him a delicious chill. "You're right. That wasn't our problem." She smiled at him, fluttering her eyelashes. "It was just so complicated between us, wasn't it?"

"Yes," said Owen, looking into her eyes. *No,* he thought.

She pulled her hand from his, gently reaching down and patting him on the knee. Owen felt that familiar wrenching in his gut and that familiar expansion in his slacks. *Oh, Christ, not now*, he said to himself, willing the hard-on into submission. He smiled crookedly and thought about his teacher from sixth grade. Mrs. Wankowski. She was built like a tank and was mean as a dog. That always worked. Owen took a deep breath and gratefully smoothed down his slacks. He took a gulp of ice water.

Violet was fiddling absently with her spoon. "Well, I've started seeing this new therapist, Yolanda. She's awesome," Violet began.

Oh sweet Christ, Owen thought, willing himself to not roll his eyes by looking down into his coffee cup.

"Anyhow, I told Yolanda everything—you know, about my mom and my marriages—" She looked up into Owen's startled face. "Oh, don't worry!" she said brightly. "I only had the best things to say about you, Owen. You know, how we became friends after the fact, and how understanding you are about the divorce and just how, well, grown-up you've been about everything. So many men are immature. That's what Yolanda says."

"Mmmm hmmm." Owen was noncommittal.

"She gave me these things to work on . . . you know, exercises.

Some journaling and some free-form kind of drawing things, al-though God knows I am no artist. Apparently Yolanda studied with some psychiatrist in Germany on how to interpret art from the colors and movements of the pencils and things on the page, or something."

Owen nodded, sipping his coffee. It sounded hokey. He won-dered how much Marshall had paid per hour for his wife to scrib-ble on newsprint. The waitress came over and took their orders, chicken Caesar salads, their usual.

Violet sipped at her herbal iced tea. "I'm going to work really hard, Owen, on me for a change, you know? I guess Marshall saw it as kind of selfish. He hated it when I was seeing Dr. Coulter. He said it was too expensive, but I know he was just . . . you know, threatened. And he was so jealous."

Wow, Owen thought, mentally ticking off Marshall's nega-tive traits—unhappy, judgmental, jealous—what would be next? Violet pushed her hair back behind her ear, and despite his cyni-cism about her, Owen found the gesture youthful and charming. He smiled at Violet, encouraging her to continue. "You know, I went to this retreat up at Higgins Lake. Marshall was so mad. He accused me of seeing someone! Can you imagine it?"

"No," said Owen. *Yes!* he thought.

"Well, he did!" Violet sat back, folding her arms over her chest. "Like I would want to become involved with any of those losers from the therapy group! Can you imagine?"

"Absolutely not," said Owen, thinking about crazy "Hubcap" Jankowicz up in the backwoods of Omer. His chrome-covered abode was legend. There'd even been a small-town newspaper story about it. That had had a recycling angle to it, though, not the this-guy-went-nuts-after-his-wife-left-him angle. Owen won-dered, and not for the first time, if Jankowicz thought nailing all those hubcaps to his house kept the Martians out or something, like some people thought wrapping their heads or covering their windows with tin foil (shiny side out!) deflected gamma rays.

Violet was still talking about her therapist, The New and Great Yolanda. He'd kind of nodded out, though he appeared to be paying attention. He'd gotten good at it. He'd also heard this schtick a least a hundred times before, not to mention that he took his turn paying for it. *How can any one person need so much therapy*, he thought, *and never get normal?* "Marshall and I started fighting about it—the money. He said all therapy was doing was causing problems between us. He couldn't see that I was growing, you know? At the Center they called it Becoming The Self. See, I was growing and changing, and Marshall wasn't. I mean, not that he's not a nice enough guy, but you can't stay stagnant, you know? That's always a disaster for a relationship." She picked at her salad with her fork. She hadn't eaten a bite.

"Sure. Sure." Owen was nearly done with his salad. He'd spent the whole time chewing, nodding, *mmm hmmm*ing. Just like old times. He looked at his watch. He had to be getting back to the office soon. If he didn't have those files updated by Monday morning, Shelly, his office manager, had threatened to neuter him. "So, what happened?" he said, wanting to expedite the conversation to the actual breakup. "Why'd you leave?"

Violet sighed. "Oh," she said, winding up for another long conversation. "It was a long time coming." Owen pointed to his watch. "Oh . . . sorry. You have to get back." He smiled indulgently.

"We had this giant blow up. I mean, Marshall was yelling and throwing stuff and everything. And you know, Owen, I will just not tolerate violence of any kind. I told him I was no good for him and that I should leave."

Owen's fork clattered onto his plate. "Violet, are you fucking kidding me?" He leaned forward on both hands. "That card again? 'I'm no good for you?' How many times do you think you can pull that old shoe out? For once why don't you say what you really mean?"

Violet's hand fluttered to her throat. "Owen!" she hissed, looking around to see if anyone was watching them. "Shhhh! And what do you mean, say what I really mean? I am an open-minded person, and Yolanda says—"

"Oh, I don't give a fat fucking fig what Yolanda says. I imagine it's akin to what Dr. Coulter told you when you were married to Winston, and what Harvey Shinmann told you after you and Hubca— I mean, Brian, broke up, and what your encounter group leader said, and yadda yadda. What you mean, Violet, is Marshall is no longer good for you." Owen's face had gone pink, and he could tell his blood pressure was up. "He was disposable! Just like I was!" *Fuck*, he said to himself. *Oh, fucking fuck.*

Violet wiped her mouth and put her napkin over her untouched salad. She put her hands in her lap and straightened her back. "Well. I just can't believe you are so hostile, Owen. And we've been such good friends, too."

"Yeah, about that," Owen began.

"Yes?" Violet said, arching her eyebrow. Her voice was frosty. *Oh, yes,* Owen thought, *I remember it well.*

Owen had no idea why he was suddenly so angry. What did he care if Violet had left Marshall? Didn't that open up a window for him, possibly? He could suddenly hear his mother in his head. *You really want to go through that again, Owen? You are an idiot, just like your father.* He took a deep breath and looked at Violet. "Never mind," he said.

"Never mind?"

"Yes, Violet. Let's not go there, okay? I have to get back to the office anyway."

Violet rolled her eyes. "On a Sunday?"

"Case notes," he said, a little more pointedly than he meant to, but deep down, he resented having to explain.

Violet looked down into her lap. "Well, okay," she sniffed. Then she looked up at Owen. It was plain that she didn't believe him. "I understand. I know you have some feelings for me you haven't resolved, and this is uncomfortable for you. You know," she leaned forward and lowered her voice. "You could probably benefit from some therapy yourself."

Owen scooted his chair back and tipped his head at her. He threw some money on the table for the lunch. "Talk to you later, Violet," he said. *You have absofreakinlutely no idea, you crazy broad*, he thought.

chapter 9

Brian "Hubcap" Jankowicz hunkered down and peered through the peephole in his front door. There were two dudes on the porch. One was a big guy with curly black hair, graying at the temples. He had a gray soul patch, and what looked like a day's worth of beard. His hands were jammed into the pockets of his black leather jacket, which he wore over a plain white T-shirt. He looked decidedly uncomfortable.

The other man was medium height, thin, and well dressed. His light brown hair was short and brushed back on the side, and he had a light scruff of beard on his face. He had a sport jacket over his blue button-down shirt. He looked out of place standing on the porch in the middle of nowhere in a way that seemed familiar to Hubcap. Both men looked a little worse for the wear. The thinner man was carrying a six-pack of Bud Light. They stood, squinting against the morning sun, which reflected off the double row of 1971 Ford LTD wheel covers nailed to the front door. Hubcap figured they were lost. He sure didn't know who they were, and certainly, no one came here to visit him. Not anymore. Except his mom, and sometimes his sister, Charla. He opened the front door a crack.

"Yeah?" he said.

"You Brian Jankowicz?" The thinner man asked.

No one called him Brian anymore. Not even his mom. "Who wants to know?" he asked, positioning his foot against the door in case he needed extra leverage to close and lock it quick. They weren't cops for sure; they had the sixer of Bud. Not that he'd done anything wrong, but who wanted to see cops on their porch?

"I'm Marsh. Marshall VanDahmm." He pointed a thumb at the bigger man. "This is Costa."

"So?" said Hubcap, wary, but he opened the door a little wider. The Bud was starting to look good. He hadn't had a beer all day, and it was getting toward noon. He was thirsty.

"We're here about Violet," the thin one said.

A sound escaped Hubcap that sounded suspiciously like a dog barking, and the door slammed shut, the windows on either side of it rattling in their frames.

"Wow," said Marshall, looking toward Costa, who was off the porch like a shot. "Hey, where you going?" he called after him.

"He's fucking nuts, man," said Costa. "And here we are, stupid *láchanos* from the city standing on his porch. He's probably going to get a gun or a rabid dog in there or something. Let's go."

"Stupid what?" Marshall said.

"*Láchanos.*" Costa said, making his hands in a ball shape. "Cabbage heads."

Marshall turned and banged his fist on the door again. "Come on, Brian!" He said. "Have a beer with us."

"You fucking nuts, too?" Costa began walking through the leaf-covered yard to the truck. "I'm outta here."

"Come on, man!" Marshall said, coming down the stairs. "Coming out here was your idea. Jeez!"

"Not to talk. Just to show you," Costa turned to the other man, holding a finger out for emphasis. "You wanna end up like that nut? Come on. We'll go back to town, eat, get on with our lives. Fuck Violet."

"What did you say?" Hubcap was suddenly in the open doorway. He pointed at Costa with a grimy finger. "You shut up. I know about you. I know how you are. Violet told me all about you!" The young man jerked his arms around in the air, his worn flannel shirt billowing out around his skinny ribs like a sail.

Costa backed away, not taking his eyes off Hubcap. "See," he said to Marshall. "You ready to go now?"

Marshall had already turned toward Hubcap. He held out his hand. "Hey, Brian," he said. "Marshall VanDahmm. Violet's sixth."

"Huh?" Hubcap looked at Marshall warily. "What do you mean?"

"Sixth husband," Marshall said. "And Costa, here, is her second." He put his hand up conspiratorially. "After Dead Winston and him, seems she went after us younger guys."

"Fuck you," said Costa.

"Stop it," Hubcap sputtered. "Stop . . . swearing!"

"Oh, what the fuck?" said Costa.

Hubcap put his hands over his ears. "I said . . . I said stop it!"

"Yeah, don't rile him up, you crazy Greek," said Marshall, grinning. Costa raised his middle finger at Marshall.

Hubcap came down the stairs. He was wearing socks that were less than pristine, and no shoes. He had on long thermal underwear that may have once been white under his red flannel shirt, and he sported holey jeans. His teeth looked like they hadn't been brushed in a coon's age. And he stank.

Marshall stepped back. "Whew, buddy, he said, waving his hand in front of his nose. "When's the last time you had a shower?"

Hubcap kept his eyes on Marshall. "My hot water heater doesn't work," he said sullenly. He licked at his chapped lips. "So, where is she?" He swallowed hard, his throat making a dry, clicking sound.

"Who? Violet?" Marshall's eyes were flinty. "Your guess is as good as mine, pal." He sat the six-pack down on the bottom step, pulled a bottle out of its sleeve, and twisted off the top. He took a long drink of beer. "She left me." His mood took a sudden downshift. "I don't know where the hell she is."

"You were married . . . to her?" Hubcap said, and Marshall nodded. "Can I . . . have one of those?" Brian looked hungrily at the bottles of beer sweating enticingly on the porch steps. Marshall pulled another beer out of the pack, handed it to Hubcap, then held another out to Costa, who came forward reluctantly and took it. The three men stood for a moment, drinking and eyeballing each other.

"She left you?" he said to Marshall, who nodded. He turned to Costa. "You too?"

"I'm over it," said Costa, waving dismissively and taking a long drink of beer.

"Really?" said Marshall, then mimicking, "'Oh, I miss the way she smells. She looks like an angel.'"

"Fuck you, you fucked-up son of a bitch," Costa spat.

"Oh, calm down," said Marshall.

"Yeah," said Hubcap. "Calm is real good."

Costa raised an eyebrow.

"You guys wanna come in?" Hubcap slid the empty back in the pack and grabbed another bottle.

"No," said Costa. "Yes," said Marshall, at the very same time.

chapter 10

Tim looked up from the computer he was working on and sighed. He ran a hand through his curly brown hair and pushed his glasses up on his nose. Mom was ringing her bell again. That fucking bell. Jenny'd gotten it for her. "Look, Mom," Jenny had said, while looking directly at Tim with squinty, mean eyes. "Isn't it pretty? I got it in Frankenmuth at that little outdoor mall. It's sterling silver."

"I hate you," Tim had said to her later as she stood at the back door putting on her coat.

"You're such a good brother," she'd returned sweetly, getting into her car, driving off, and leaving Tim to another monotonous day.

"Coming, Mom!" he called. What the fuck was he doing? Tim wondered why he'd agreed to come back to Michigan almost a year ago to take care of his parents, but he knew it was guilt. Jenny had learned the skill well from Mom. They had such a sneaky way of making you feel guilty, saying something that on the surface seemed nice or maybe even inconsequential, but underneath . . . If a stranger were standing there listening to the conversation he'd never understand the dastardliness of what was going on. Jenny could tell him he was a great brother, but what she really meant was, you would be a great brother except for you left me here to take care of Mom and Dad while you licked your wounds in Indiana and now I don't have a relationship or any friends or an education or a life. But that's okay, bro. No problem, man.

"Where you going?" his dad called from the living room as Tim walked by."Mom rang the bell, Dad." Tim said.

"Huh?"

"The bell!" Tim said loudly. "Mom is ringing!" The bell went off again, insistently. Tim's dad never heard the bell. He refused to wear his hearing aid. Tim wondered, not for the first time, if his dad wasn't the smartest person in the whole damn household.

"Coming, Mom!" he called out loudly. She wouldn't wear her hearing aid, either. Too much of a bother, she always said.

"Hey, Mom," Tim said. His mother's room was a pigsty, full of old magazines, knickknacks, books, junk mail and photographs. The volume on the television boomed in the small room. She sat up in her bed, wearing a ruffled bed jacket, her glasses perched on her nose, squinting at Judge Judy.

"That Judge Judy knows how to flip the flapjacks," his mom hollered. "She doesn't let those bums get away with anything."

"What did you need, Mom?" Tim asked.

"What?"

Tim sighed and reached for the remote. He muted the set. "What do you need?" he asked again.

"Oh," she said, blinking. "Oh." Tim sighed. She'd forgotten again. "What are you doing out there?" she asked.

"Working on a computer," Tim said.

"Whose computer?"

"Mom," Tim took a breath to calm himself. "Can I get you something?"

"You need to get a job," his mother said. Tim sat down on the chair beside her bed. It was full of papers, and they crunched under his ass.

"Don't mess those up!" She said. "That's my Publisher's Clearing House! I already won! I just have to send in the papers!"

Tim picked up the stack of junk mail. He was going to have to start sorting this kind of thing out of the mail before bringing it in to her. "Mom, that's all fake. We've talked about it before."

"*You've* talked about it," she said, her eyes going beady and mean. "You'll see. All of you will."

"Okay, Mom," Tim shook his head. He was never going to get his repair work done on time, though he had to admit, his customers were really understanding. Most thought it was "sweet" that he cared for his parents. His mom snatched the remote and punched the mute button. The raspy voice of Judge Judy filled the room once again. "So, you don't need anything?" Tim said loudly.

"You don't need to yell at me." She scrunched her eyes up at him. "Why are you wearing that shirt?"

Tim looked down at the T-shirt that covered his paunchy frame. A wild-haired Albert Einstein photo was emblazoned on the front.

"It's not very professional." She turned her attention back to the television.

Tim sighed. "Mom. I'm not yelling. You rang your bell. I . . ." Tim shook his head. "Look, Mom, sorry. Do you want a glass of milk and some graham crackers or something?"

Tim's mother smiled sweetly at him. "That would be nice." She reached out and patted him on the arm. "You're such a good son, Tim, taking a break from your work to come in and check on me."

"Thanks, Mom. Any time."

He trudged down the hall to the kitchen. "Fuck you, Jenny," he said aloud.

chapter 11

Costa left for Omer to pick up some more beer, and while he was gone, Marshall persuaded Hubcap to take a shower and change his clothes. Sitting in Hubcap's living room, Marshall was privy to something most Omerites—except for Hubcap's mom and perhaps his sisters—didn't know. Not only was the outside of the house swathed in wheel covers; now Hubcap was working on the inside of the house.

There seemed to be a method to his madness, though. He was kind of an artist, really, when you took a good look at his handiwork. The living room, for example, was done in a bulls-eye pattern of alternating Honda Civic and Toyota Corolla wheel covers. Prior to hanging the hubcaps, the walls had been painted a deep blue. It was kind of cool, in a creepy, weird sort of way. Maybe Marshall would let Hubcap do a wall in his living room, now that he was the sole decorator. His soon-to-be-ex would love that, wouldn't she? *Fuck you, Violet,* he thought to himself.

For all the weirdness with the hubcaps and the less-than-perfect personal hygiene, the inside of Hubcap's house was clean and organized. The carpeting appeared to be recently vacuumed, clean dishes were stacked in the drainer in a sink, and the rooms were orderly, if a bit run down. It seemed the guy cared more about the house than he did about himself.

Brian emerged from the bathroom in a cloud of steam. He had on a pair of clean jeans, and his feet were bare and pink. He'd shaved, and his face looked youngish and bloated. It was apparent he'd been drinking too much. He was thin, except for a little soft potbelly that hung dejectedly over the waistband of his pants. He was rubbing his wet hair with a holey towel.

"Where's your friend?" Brian asked.

"Went to pick up some more beer," Marshall said, draining his bottle. "And he's not exactly my friend."

Marshall outlined what had happened over the past few days, about Violet leaving him, his thinking she had someone on the side—why else would she give him such a piss-poor excuse for getting a divorce? She was no good for him? She was making him unhappy? He'd had no idea he was that unhappy until she told him he was. About how he'd heard that she'd gone to Costa months back, supposedly looking for a job. Now, why would she do something like that? Work for her ex-husband? According to Costa, she wouldn't lift a finger in the restaurant when they were married.

Marshall told Brian how he'd been sure she and Costa were seeing each other. That she had these therapy appointments and that she'd started coming home later and later. She said it was the group. The therapy. That she was supporting her group mates. That they'd meet for coffee. To Marshall she seemed secretive. It gave him a bad feeling in the pit of his stomach.

Then, just like that, she'd left. Took everything she'd wanted from their house. Marshall called in to work, drank for a few days, then went looking for Costa.

"You smashed his place up, and he still fed you and stuff?" Brian said. He sat across from Marshall in a beat-up La-Z-Boy. It was mauve. Marshall could have bet Violet had picked it out.

"Yeah." Marshall felt the sting of shame from Brian's words.

"Sounds like a friend to me," Brian said.

"Maybe."

Costa came in carrying a twelve this time, and a steaming pizza from Beanies.

"Cool," said Brian.

"Hey," said Costa. "You godda eat."

Costa cleared off a spot on the sofa and sat down next to Marshall. "So, what you boys been talking about?"

"The fact that Marshall thought Violet was cheating on him with you," Brian said bluntly.

Marshall looked down into his lap. He was thinking again how the Greek had made him breakfast, patched him up. That what Costa'd tried to do today was well intentioned.

"No worries," said Costa, slapping Marshall on the back. "Nothing you didn't say to me yourself twenty times Friday night. Good thing for you Angelina was home with the kids. If she'da heard you, she would have gone fucking ballistic and I woulda had to kick your ass for real."

Marshall leaned over, elbows on his knees, clasping his beer between his hands. "So, were you?" he asked Costa.

"Was I? Was I what?"

Marshall looked up at him, his eyes narrowing. "Well, you never really said one way or the other, now did you?"

"You think I was seeing Violet?" Costa began to laugh. "You still haven't let go of that? Are you kidding?"

"No, man. I'm not."

Brian leaned forward in his chair. This was the best drama he'd seen since his cable got turned off three weeks prior when he'd forgotten to pay his bill.

"Jesus Christ," Costa said, slapping his slice of pizza down on the top of the pizza box and his beer bottle on the table with a *thunk*. He stood up, slid his meaty hand in the pocket of his jeans, and extracted a beat-up wallet. He flipped it open and held it out for Marshall. "Look at that," he said.

Marshall took the wallet, which had been flipped open to the first picture sleeve. In it was a photograph of a gorgeous woman, a little on the plump side, but incredibly pretty, with long, wavy black hair, flashing eyes, golden skin. Her cheeks and lips seemed to be the same rosy shade of pink. On her lap were two small children, a little girl with long dark hair that looked to be about five, and a toddler, a little boy with Costa's smiling eyes. Like their mother, they were beautiful. The beautiful family was smiling into the camera.

"You think I wanna mess that up?" Costa said.

Marshall handed the wallet back to Costa. "They're . . . they're gorgeous, man."

"Thank you." Costa pocketed his wallet, sat back down on the sofa, and began eating his slice in great, wolf-like bites.

"Did you ever want to have kids?" Brian asked Marshall. "With Violet?"

Marshall sighed, sticking his long legs out under the coffee table. "I didn't think about it," Marshall said. "I knew from the get-go she couldn't. So, I just never thought about it."

"But didn't you want to?" Brian looked away, then said quietly, "She would have been a good mom."

Marshall thought about holidays at his mom's house and his

brother's kids running around, climbing on him, wanting him to play. He always felt awkward about it. But it was kind of good, too. "Yeah, maybe," he said.

"I wanted kids," Brian said. "She didn't tell me till after we were married. I was pretty unhappy about it. A little mad, too. My mom—she was really pissed."

"I hear that," said Costa, toasting Brian with his bottle.

"Your mom, too?" Brian asked Costa.

"Hey, we're Greek."

Brian nodded, not exactly sure what that meant or had to do with the question, but deciding that it sounded serious.

The men sat in silence for a while, no one knowing quite what to say.

"So, what did you come out here for?" Brian looked uncertainly at the two other men.

"Support group," Marshall said.

"Huh?"

"We're Violet's survivors." Marshall laughed. Then wryly, "At least I think I'm going to survive."

"You will," said Costa. "You just godda get your head outta your ass." He set down his empty and fished another beer out of the package. "And you, too." He pointed a finger at Brian. "What the fuck is up with this hubcap business?"

Brian's face turned so red it was nearly purple. "I don't want to talk about it."

"You have to," Marshall said. "First rule of the support group—"

"Share honestly," Marshall and Costa said together, mimicking a Violet-ism.

"I never asked to be in your stupid group."

"Who did?" said Costa, laughing.

"I don't want to talk about her." Brian curled up in the La-Z-Boy, looking like an eight-year-old in time-out.

"Suit yourself, man," said Marshall. "We're just here to help."

"We are?" said Costa. "I just drove you out here to see."

"See what?" asked Brian.

"Your crazy hubcap ass," said Costa. "Really. What's up with that?"

Brian mumbled something under his breath. Costa leaned forward, squinting. "Whachoo say?" he asked.

"I said you wouldn't understand."

"Really?" said Costa. "I was married to the crazy *kounéli*."

Brian leaned forward in his chair. "What does that mean?" he said, his eyes narrowing.

"What?" Costa spread his big hands out. "What do you care?"

"What does it mean?" Brian insisted.

"Nothing. *Kounéli*. Rabbit. You know, cute, fuzzy."

"Why do you care?" Marshall said. "She obviously fucked you up."

"You don't know that that's true," Brian said. "I was screwed up before. Always have been."

"What's wrong with you?" Costa said. "And I still godda know about the hubcaps."

"Bi-polar," Brian said, looking down at the floor.

"So what?" Marshall said. "That's just bullshit. Do you know how common that is? Bi-polar, depression, fucking Asperger's—there's medication, man. Otherwise seventy-five percent of the fucking population would be living in houses covered in hubcaps and tin foil and gum wrappers. I'm assuming you have medication?"

Brian shrugged. He wouldn't look Marshall in the eye. "Yeah," he said.

Costa smacked Marshall in the arm. He was watching Brian intently. "Cuddit out," he said.

"What?" Marshall said, popping another beer open. "The guy's got a treatable condition, he knows the diagnosis, meaning he has medication, which makes him relatively normal, whatever that means. So, this hubcap-hermit thing is a direct result of hurricane Violet."

"I said stop," said Costa. Brian was gripping the arms of the chair, his knuckles turning white. "You don't take your medicine, do you?"

Brian was still looking at the floor. "Sometimes," Brian said.

"See?" said Costa to Marshall.

"I didn't tell her either," Brian said.

"Tell who what?" Costa asked.

"I didn't tell Violet," he said. "That I was nutso. Till after we were married."

"Well, she didn't tell you she couldn't have kids either, so you were even," said Marshall.

"Not really." Brian looked up at the other men. He pushed his damp hair back with his palm, exposing a receding hairline. "I . . . wanted kids but . . . I didn't, too." He looked at Costa. "I was scared that I could pass on what I got. You understand, right?"

"Sure. Sure." Costa thought of his own children at home and the ways they were like both him and Angelina. Danny had Angie's quick temper, and little Andrea had her father's light-hearted nature. He bobbed his head at Marshall. "He's still pissed. It's fresh for him."

"Right," said Brian. He sat thinking for a moment. "So," he said. "Dead Winston was her first husband, Costa was number two, I was third, and Marshall was number six?"

"Yeah," said Marshall. "Pretty fucking messed up, isn't it?"

"What happened to the other two guys?" Brian asked.

PROGRESS NOTES: Violet VanDahmm
    CASE NUMBER: V2011-100982
    DATE: 10-06-2011

SUMMARY:

We began the appointment defining Violet's multiple relationships. When asked to describe each of her ex-husbands using only one word, Violet replied easily and quickly (Winston: distinguished, Costa: strong, Brian: damaged, Tim: smart, Marshall: handsome). When I informed her she had skipped Owen, Violet became somewhat distraught. She replied that she would have described Owen with the word "friend," but that they had a recent disagreement and she was unclear as to whether or not they were friends any longer.

When asked whether Violet has maintained congenial relationships with any of her other exes, she said she had not. I asked her what she thought it was about Owen that made it possible for them to remain friends after their divorce. She replied, "I don't know, really. We weren't friends at first; he was terribly hurt after the breakup. Then we ran into one another one night at a restaurant, and I guess I just made him talk to me." I asked her how she accomplished this, and she smiled rather coquettishly. "Oh, he still thinks he is in love with me; it wasn't hard." Violet then launched into a rather lengthy discussion about the disagreement with Owen, and she used several therapeutic terms to describe his problems as related to their friendship/relationship. Efforts to refocus the conversation on Violet's issues resulted in making the client defensive and sullen.

For a journal assignment, I suggested that Violet focus this week on her first experiences with love and relationships, to be used in discussion at our following appointment.

Yolanda H. Malik, LCSW
Champoor and Associates

chapter 12

Owen wasn't sure about this. It felt . . . somehow disloyal to Violet. He was torn. Their last meeting still weighed heavy on his mind, the way he'd snapped when she told him she'd left Marshall, the feelings that had churned up. Had she said the same thing to all of them? It's not you, it's me? Except for Dead Winston, that was. And Jake.

Owen got just as tired of hearing about Jake as he'd been of hearing about Violet's many forays into therapy, which were extensive. *Violet changed therapists as often as she changed husbands*, he thought. According to Violet, Jake was her high school sweetheart. She had a big box of Jake-o-mobelia, as Owen liked to call it, that she kept accessible on a closet shelf. Notes they'd passed back and forth in class, tickets to concerts they went to, high school newspaper pictures, drawings, even a coffee spoon from the first time they had coffee together. Never washed, for God's sake. Whenever she'd been feeling particularly vulnerable or maudlin, she'd get the box out, sit on the bed she shared with Owen, and rummage through it all. The sad look she'd gotten in her eyes tore at Owen. When they were together, Owen often wondered if she would get that look on her face when she thought about him if they ever split up.

Thing was, Jake and Violet had never dated. Violet claimed she'd been "violently in love" with him, but he'd just wanted to be friends. She carried her torch throughout her whole four years of high school and beyond. She never forgot him, went to every high school reunion, hoping to see him, dragging whichever husband she was married to at the time with her, but Jake seemed to have disappeared off the face of the earth. None of their old crowd knew anything about him, where he'd gone, whether or not he was married, had kids, what field he worked in. Owen remembered the dejected look on her face after the reunion he'd attended with her. Afterward, she'd taken the Jake-o-mobelia box off the closet shelf and shoved it under her side of the bed.

After high school, they'd written to each other for a while, when Jake was in the service. Violet had saved all his letters and kept them tied up with a piece of lavender satin ribbon in her panty drawer. Owen remembered fighting that losing battle, trying to get her to throw them out. Telling her how it made him feel to know his wife was hoarding letters from another guy in her underwear drawer. But Violet had given him the cold shoulder, pouted that he didn't understand her or her feelings, and she kept the letters. Violet refused to let go of her Jake.

Owen wondered what it was about this guy had that so attracted Violet, and also wondered how the guy had had the willpower to resist Violet's wiles. She had a way of getting what she wanted. It was those eyes, and the way she would snuggle up close, pressing her breasts into your arm or chest, the way she smelled, and the way she always seemed to know the thing to say to get right under your skin. His grandfather would have called her a vixen.

He pulled into the parking lot of Plati Pavlos. It was packed—an indication that the food here must be pretty good. He spied an open spot and was about to pull in when a late-model Jeep Cherokee zipped around a corner and pulled in ahead of him. Owen slammed on his brakes, hitting the button to roll down the window to yell at the guy, but the asshole was already out of his car and heading toward the door at a fast clip. Owen got a glimpse of curly, thinning hair. He swore under his breath and made his way toward the back edge of the lot.

Owen sat in the SUV, deciding whether or not he wanted to go in. When Marshall VanDahmm called him in the middle of the week, he'd been wary, but they were soon chatting it up like old chums. He was a nice guy, a graphic designer, and they'd even gotten to talking about Marsh designing some new business cards and pamphlets for Owen's veterinary business. Marsh said he could cut Owen a deal.

Talking with Marsh was great, but the other guys? Violet had told him enough about Costa to make him sure he didn't want to meet him, about his vulgarity, his family, the way they'd treated Violet, made her feel horrible about her inability to bear a child. That was just low.

He knew virtually nothing about Brian Jankowicz. Violet refused to talk about him, and in fact seemed embarrassed to even mention his name. The other guy, Tim Stark, had been so torn up over his divorce from Violet that he'd left the state so he wouldn't have to run into her. Violet had described it as "tragic" and hoped he would "look within and heal his inner child" so he could "get past his mother issues" and have a healthy relationship. Another case of husbandly non-growth. Owen wondered, and not for the first time, how she'd portrayed him after their divorce, and he decided that was just a bad road to go down.

Well, he was here. Might as well go in and have some dinner. He liked Greek food, and if things got too weird, he was prepared. He'd asked Shelly to page him around eight o'clock so he'd have an excuse to leave the table and decide whether or not he needed to run out because of an "emergency."

Owen stepped into Palati Pavlos and was greeted at the door by a pretty young lady who offered to hang up his jacket. There was a man ahead of him at the reception desk, looking decidedly uncomfortable. "I'm meeting someone?" he said noncommittally. Owen narrowed his eyes. It was the asshole that had stolen his parking space.

Owen stepped closer. He tapped the guy on the shoulder.

"What's the name of your party?" The hostess opened her reservation book.

The guy turned to Owen. "Yeah?"

"You the guy in the Jeep?" Owen said. "You took my parking spot."

"Sir . . . your party?"

"Um . . . VanDahmm?" said the man distractedly, keeping his eyes on Owen. "I got the spot before you—don't know what to tell you." He turned away from Owen.

Owen was about to tap the guy on the shoulder again when the name registered. "Wait—did you say VanDahmm?"

"Yeah, so?" The guy was starting to look irritated. He was bigger than Owen, and when he turned to looked at him, Owen stepped back a little. The hostess looked from one to the other of them nervously.

"That's . . . um . . . that's me, too." Owen regarded the guy— medium build, a little on the heavy side, with curly brown hair and green eyes encased in wire-rimmed glasses. He was wearing a corduroy jacket over nicely pressed jeans and a black T-shirt. Owen stuck his hand out, and the guy took it reluctantly. "I believe we're at the same table. I'm Owen Blanton."

"Tim Stark," the other man said, eyeing him. "So, you're the vet." He had a solid grip and shook Owen's hand heartily. "Animal doc, I mean—not veteran. I mean, unless you are. A veteran. Geez." He wiped at his brow. "Sorry, man," Tim said. "I'm as nervous as a schoolgirl on her first date."

"I don't think they're quite that nervous, Tim," Owen said, grinning despite himself. No use getting off on the wrong foot.

"No?"

"Think about it. They hold all the cards. And they know it."

"Well, you've got that right," Tim said.

Owen looked apologetically at the hostess. She shook her head at them. "This way," she said, sidling around in front of them. She lead them through the dining room to a private booth near the back of the restaurant.

Marshall stood up and greeted them. "Must be Owen and Tim," he said, reaching out to shake both their hands. "This is Brian." Brian nodded, nervously. This was the fanciest restaurant he'd ever been in, and he hoped he was dressed okay. He hadn't wanted to ask his mom or Charla about it because they'd bitch if he mentioned anything about Violet. "Costa will be right out. Says he's making us something special," Marshall continued.

A waitress came and took drink orders, and the men began a careful conversation that stuck to their jobs, cars, and sports. After about twenty minutes, the Greek himself joined them. Costa approached the table, his face shiny with sweat, the smells of the kitchen emanating off his white apron.

"You boys doing good?" He wiped his hands on a dishtowel.

"Yeah, we're fine, Costa," said Marshall, and he introduced him to Tim and Owen.

"Ready to eat?" Costa had a big grin on his face. "We are going to have a feast, okay?" He gestured to two of the waitresses standing at the ready near the kitchen door, and he sat down with the other men. "One rule," he said. "No talk of you-know-who in my place, eh? And anyway, it's no good for digestion."

There were nods of agreement, and privately more than a little relief. None of the men were quite ready to talk about Violet. They'd kept their pain, disappointment, and embarrassment essentially private. They'd all felt like fools. The more time it took to eat, the better.

They filled up on giant Greek salads full of pepperoncinis, olives, beets, and feta cheese; roasted lamb with little potatoes sprinkled with oregano, thyme, and olive oil; slices of spanakopita; and many glasses of Porto Carras. Afterward there were plates of baklava, redolent with honey and walnuts, and big, steaming mugs of tea with lemon and honey. Costa's pretty waitresses were attentive, complimenting and flirting with the men. It was the best meal any of them remembered having in a long time.

By the time the men got to Johnny's Pub down the street, they were well on their way to a good drunk. Costa ordered a round of shots to start them off.

"No way, Costa, come on," said Marshall. "After that meal? You've been more than generous, man."

"No kidding," Owen agreed. "That was truly magnificent."

"Hey, it's what I do," said Costa. He was grinning ear to ear with pride.

"Surprised Violet didn't weigh two hundred pounds after being married to you," Tim said, letting out a healthy belch. Everyone laughed.

Costa waved his hand. "Ah, she hardly came in the restaurant. Now, the club, that was her thing.

"What club?" Brian asked.

"Was next door to the restaurant. Me and Angie closed it down. Too much fighting. Gangs. Shit like that. We wanted to keep the restaurant more family, you know?"

"Yeah," said Brian.

Owen turned and smacked Tim on the arm. "So, how'd Marshall find you? Least I assume it was Marsh."

Marshall took a mock bow.

"LinkedIn," said Tim. "He knew I was a computer geek, so he started poking around. Although I have to say," he pointed at Marshall, "I wasn't sure I was going to respond."

"Ah, the intrigue of Violet," Marshall said, taking a sip of his drink.

"Whatever, man," said Tim.

"So, what'd the message say?" asked Owen.

"This was great," said Marshall, getting a shit-eating grin on his face. "Do you miss Violet Benjamin Montgomery Pavlos Jankowicz Blanton Stark VanDahmm?"

"Seriously?" said Owen.

"Seriously," Tim answered. "At first I wondered, you know, was it, you know, Violet screwing around? She is one head-fucking broad. And I wasn't going to do anything about it. But I hedged my bets and Marsh here emailed me back and told me about the . . . uh . . . support group."

"You are seriously calling this a support group?" Owen asked Marshall.

"What else would you call it?"

"I don't know. Support group sounds femmy."

"Men go to support groups."

"Whatever, man," Owen signaled the bartender for another round. Brian looked uneasy. He shifted nervously in his chair and kept glancing toward the door. "What's the matter with you?" Owen asked Brian.

"Look, you guys all live close and I have to get back up home. Plus, I am kinda . . . unemployed right now so . . ."

"No worries." Costa said, clapping him on the back. "You stay at our place tonight, okay?"

"No, I—"

"Sonny boy, you turning down my hospitality?" Brian shrugged. "Good," said Costa. "It's settled."

"I have a question," said Tim.

"Shoot," said Marshall.

Tim looked at Costa. "So, if I have this right, you're the only one of us who is remarried. In fact, the only one of us who actually has a relationship with a woman." He looked at the other men. "Am I right? Well, Marsh, you don't count. Too new. Unless you're a big whore and went right out and boned some women."

"No boning to date to report," said Marshall.

"What about you, Owen?" Tim asked.

Owen shifted uncomfortably in his seat. He didn't want to tell them he still saw Violet, that they were friends. That she was the only steady female companionship he'd had since the divorce. Other than a few one-nighters that never worked into anything more. He threw up his hands helplessly. "Yep. No girlfriend."

"And sonny boy, here, has been too busy decorating for space invaders to think about women, right?" Costa clasped Brian around the shoulders, and the younger man turned a deep shade of red. Costa gave him a brotherly squeeze. "Don't worry aboudit. S'all good."

Brian smiled wanly.

"So, what's your secret?" Tim asked Costa.

"Secret?"

"Yeah," Tim said. "You seem to be happy. Got two nice little kids. How'd you do that?"

"Yeah, how'd you get over her?" Brian wanted to know.

Costa leaned forward on a hairy forearm and took a drink. He looked up at the other men. "You know," he said. "I could sit here and act like a big man and tell you it was easy." He looked down at the table. "But truth is, it wasn't. I nearly lost everything being a big, stupid *ilíthios*. This is the way it was."

✳ ✳ ✳

Costa knew he was in trouble when Niki sent Olivia instead of coming himself. Olivia was half Greek and half Italian and not a woman to trifle with. She let herself in with the key Niki gave her and started screaming for Costa the minute she was in the door of the now-filthy house.

"Where are you?" she yelled, slamming her way through the house. "Costa Pavlos! Look at this place! Filthy pig!" She made her way through the kitchen and living room, swearing all the way, and into the den where Costa was sleeping. "Oh, my God! Your mamma would have a fit!"

Costa was lying half on and half off the pullout sofa. He was naked. When he heard Olivia shrieking, he covered his head with a pillow and went back to sleep, ignoring the stinking pocket of air his horrid breath made under the pillow. He hadn't washed in days, and the room, which hadn't been aired out since Violet had left weeks before, was rancid.

Olivia came into the room, holding her wool scarf over her nose, swearing in a combination of Greek and Italian. She screeched at the sight of Costa's nude, hairy ass and began beating it with one of the newspapers she'd rescued from the stoop. The soggy roll of newsprint made a hollow *swack-swack* as she smacked.

"Get up, you dirty, disgusting pig!" Olivia said. "Look at you! Like an animal!"

"Fuck off," Costa mumbled into the mattress.

Olivia drew in a self-righteous breath. "Is that how you talk to a lady?" she demanded.

"No!" Costa hollered from under his pillow. "So, fuck off!"

Olivia growled and snatched away the pillow, causing Costa's head to smack down hard on the metal frame of the hide-a-bed. "Wait till I tell Mamma how you treat me!"

"Ow! What you tryin' to do?" Costa whined.

"Get up! Right now!" Olivia said. "I can't believe you, Costa! After everything Niki's done for you! What are you doing? You have a business to run! You are leaving Niki to take care of everything! And what does he get for it but heartache, eh?"

"Okay . . . okay . . ." Costa said, rolling over and exposing his gigantic morning wood. His penis poked up in the air like a proud pup.

Olivia screamed and picked up the pillow, pushing it down on Costa's erection. "You're a dirty man."

Costa groaned and rolled to the side of the bed, throwing the pillow aside. "Bullshit," he said. "I am a man who has to take a piss." He stood up, scratching his hairy stomach and balls, and left Olivia in his stinking wake.

When he got out of the shower, wonderful smells were wafting through the house from the kitchen. Smells Costa hadn't had the stomach for in a while. Olivia had made a hole in the messy kitchen and fixed a pot of coffee. She stood at the sink, putting scummy dishes into hot, soapy water to soak. Bacon was crisping in a cast-iron skillet on the stove, and there was a saucepan of hard-boiled eggs on the warmer. Costa sat down at the table with a sigh. Olivia refused to look at him, her hands moving industriously in the dishwater.

Everything in Costa hurt. He didn't have the energy to get up. He couldn't remember where he'd gone last night. Johnny's? The Pub? He willed Olivia to bring him a cup of the aromatic coffee, and as if she heard him, she gave an indignant sniff and turned on the hot water full blast.

Costa got up from the table with a grimace and made his way to the counter. He poured a cup of steaming coffee, put it to his nose, and sniffed appreciatively.

"No one makes coffee like you, Olivia."

"Hm," was all she said.

"Well, thank you." He gave a little bow. "What time is it?" he said, making his way back to the kitchen table.

"Nearly eleven." Olivia's voice was stilted.

"Shit," Costa said.

Olivia turned like a whirling dervish. "Shit is right, Costa!" she said shrilly. "Almost lunch rush! And where are you? Again?" She didn't wait for him to answer. "That's right! Sitting here in your own drunken filth and leaving my Niki to deal with everything? You know what else, Costa? When you do this shit, I have to be there practically twenty-four-seven to help him! And who do you think is taking care of my kids?"

"I'm sorry, Olivia," Costa said, hanging his head.

"Mamma! That's who!" she said, as if he'd remained silent. "Sorry? You're sorry? None of the bills for the restaurant are paid, Costa!" She smacked him on the shoulder and he winced, pain shooting through his head. "People are calling. They're pissed off!

They are telling Niki they aren't gonna bring the orders. What the fuck are you doing?"

Olivia sat down next to him and grabbed his face in her hand the way his mamma used to when he did something bad. "What are you doing?" she repeated, and Costa could now see she had tears in her eyes. Tears for him. "That woman was no wife to you, and here you sit throwing your life and your livelihood away because of her? Do you think she cares, Costa? Get your head out of your big Greek ass. She's gone. And good for you! You don't see a blessing when it smacks you in your big dumb face?"

She stood up, but her face was very close to his. She reached up and wiped at her eyes with the dishtowel. "If you don't stop this, Niki and I are leaving. We are not cleaning up your mess anymore. And I'm calling your mamma."

Now Costa was truly scared. His eyes went wide, and he began to sweat. He grabbed Olivia's hand. "Don't do that!" he said. "Jesus, Olivia."

"Do you think I want to? You know how she treats me. No woman is ever good enough for 'her boys.'" Olivia rolled her eyes. "But if you don't get dressed, to hell with it, I'm calling her. And you come to the restaurant and take care of things. You better be there in an hour," Olivia told him. "Or else."

At the restaurant, Niki was tight-lipped and the waitresses wouldn't look Costa in the eye. Red-faced, he grabbed a clean apron off the shelf, donned it, and began scrubbing his hands at the wash station. He joined Niki at the grill, grabbed a couple of tickets, and started putting plates together. The two men worked side by side in silence for a while.

Finally, Niki spoke. "What I really need you to do is get the office stuff in shape. Me and Olivia tried to sort it out, but there are some things that just need your attention. I can handle lunch. Dinner too, far as that goes."

"Yeah?" It felt out of place to have someone else tell him what needed to be done in his own restaurant, but Costa nodded in agreement.

"And we're behind paying the girls," Niki said. "Do that first so none of them walk." Niki shot Costa a grin. "Especially the good-looking ones, eh?"

"Sure," said Costa. No wonder the girls wouldn't look at him. They were a good staff, too, for the most part. That was hard to come by. He felt like a heel.

"Olivia gave them some cash," Niki told them. "She wrote it all down. You'll have to figure out what you still owe them."

Costa looked at his cousin, then down at his shoes. "Nik," he said. "I'm sorry, man."

"I know, bro. Me too. We gotta get things back on track though, you know?" Niki put plates up in the window and pulled two of the tickets down, placing them on a spike near the grill, then started on the next tickets.

Costa headed to his office and sat at his trashed desk, berating himself for not adding Niki to the accounts so he could take care of things just in case. He shook his head. He was being just like his father used to be, not trusting anybody but himself. Look where that got him. Early grave. Heart attack. Costa made himself a mental note to take Niki down to the bank and get him on the signature cards. Maybe Olivia, too.

The books were a mess. Costa'd been coming in and taking cash, spending. On stupid things. Drinking a lot. He'd been to the casino a few times, bought some clothes. The biggest purchase however, was the motorcycle. It was a 1962 Norton 650SS that he bought from a guy in Detroit for $6,800. In cash. He hadn't been writing anything down. As Costa flipped through receipts and invoices and deposit slips, his stomach knotted and he began to sweat. In the checkbook he found a receipt for a check he'd written to Violet dated several weeks prior, which he didn't remember writing, for five thousand dollars. What the hell? Why did he do that? After she was the one who left him? He sure didn't want to call her to find out. All he knew was he'd really fucked up.

There wasn't enough money to pay the vendors. Even with this week's anticipated revenue, he was going to come up short. He could sell the bike, maybe, but that still wasn't going to make up for his gambling and drinking debts. He wasn't going to ask Niki for help—he'd done enough to keep Costa's ass afloat. And in any case, Olivia would slit his throat if he asked Niki for money.

Costa sighed. He leaned on his elbows, head in his hands, waiting for the wave of nausea to pass. He knew what he had to do. He was going to have to call his mother. It was the lowest point of Costa's life.

＊ ＊ ＊

"So, how'd you meet Angelina?" Marshall asked.

Costa signaled the bartender for another round of beers. "You're not gonna believe this. My mother."

"Seriously?" asked Marshall.

"As a heart attack."

Owen was laughing. "Your mom picked out your wife?"

"Hey," said Costa, turning to him. "Don't knock it. Angie is fantastic. You know, she came in here when I was all screwed up, owed people money. It felt like I was starting all over again. I had to borrow some money from my mother to keep the restaurant afloat. She told me she'd do it, but I had to hire this girl, Angelina D'Lessandro. She brought Angelina with her when she came up from Detroit. Anyhow, Angie started here as a hostess and took on more and more responsibilities with the business, helped me close down the club and sell the building. She helped get me back on track."

"You tell her about Violet?" asked Tim.

"I told her enough. She figured some stuff out, and I think Olivia told her some things. Those two are thick like thieves. But the thing she did best was love me, and then later be a good mother to my kids. She stuck by me. Still does. And kicks my ass regular." He nudged Brian. "But who cares, huh? When she loves you good later, right, sonny boy?"

Brian's face turned pink. "I guess so," he said.

"I don't know," said Tim. "I don't think I could do it."

"Do what?" Owen asked.

"Get married again." Tim was peeling the labels off his beer bottles and had made a little nest of paper on the table in front of him. "I was dating a girl for a while. Like two months. I called her Violet one night."

Marshall and Owen both sucked in a breath. "Ouch," Owen said.

"Yeah. She asked me who Violet was. In fact, she was convinced it was someone I was seeing at the same time I was seeing her. It just made it worse when I said she was my ex-wife. She stopped seeing me after that." He paused and took a drink of his beer. "What is it about Violet that turns you into a bumbling idiot?" he asked the men.

"She gets you all mixed up," said Brian. He was the only one no longer drinking, even though Costa offered to buy for him. He was nursing a tall glass of Coke.

"That's for sure," said Owen, thinking about his last lunch date with Violet. Going into it, he'd thought he was in control of the situation, but in mere minutes she'd had him all riled up. He looked at Marshall. "How about you?" he said. "You're the newest—what do you want to call it? Victim? How are you doing with all this?"

"*Victim's* a shitty word, Owen," Marshall said. "Didn't you learn anything from Violet? Don't you know that if you are a victim it's because—"

"You allowed yourself to be victimized!" Tim and Owen said in high, squeaky voices.

"Yeah, fuck both of you," Marshall said.

"Can we stop with all the f-bombs?" Brian said.

"Seriously, man?" said Marshall. "It really bothers you that much?"

"Yes. No. Yes. Kinda," Brian said.

"Sorry, dude," Marshall said.

Marshall rubbed at his forehead. He was tired. "Save my story for another time," he said. "I'm bushed." It was getting near closing. Everyone was worn out and more than a little drunk.

"So, what's next?" Owen downed the remainder of his beer and set the empty alongside the other dead soldiers on the table.

There were shrugs and *I-don't-know*s.

"Let's meet up again," Costa said.

Everyone looked at him.

"I know. I know. I thought it was crazy bullshit, too. But this was kinda nice. You're nice fellas."

There were embarrassed murmurs all around the table.

"Thanks, man."

"Yeah, thanks."

"Well, how about it?" boomed Costa. "Same time, same place, in a few weeks?"

chapter 13

That night, when Marshall got home, he noticed he was not feeling the weighty dread he'd been feeling the last few days at facing
the Violet-less rooms. He'd flown by the seat of his pants with the
support group thing, and deep down still saw it as a big joke, a
way to get back at Violet, and ultimately a way to not be alone.
Regardless of his outer toughness and nonchalance he showed to
the guys, his heart was breaking. He missed Violet.

Things like the bathroom, still smelling of her soap and
shampoo, bothered him. Some of her T-shirts and socks in the
laundry baskets she'd forgotten. Her fairy necklace hanging on a
knob on the dresser. Her mail, still being delivered to the house:
Mrs. Violet VanDahmm. He still didn't understand, and quite
honestly, he felt like a sucker. He should have known. After all, he
was her sixth husband. She was like fucking Liz Taylor.

Come to think about it, she even looked a little like Liz Tayor:
heart-shaped face, big eyes—brown though, not violet like Liz's—

black hair, the little nipped-in waist. She was full of energy and would do sweet things like remembering the shaving soap you liked best, or that you don't like green shirts, or making sure your favorite ice cream was always in the freezer, butter pecan, even though she didn't like that kind. It was nice to have someone that paid attention to the little things like that.

Marshall walked into his kitchen, which was a disaster. He hadn't been eating much, but there were some fast food wrappers on the counter, and lots of cups and glasses in the sink. Marshall wasn't tired, even though it was late and he was sure feeling the drinks he's had at Costa's place, and later at Johnny's Bar. He opened the dishwasher and started loading it. He started wondering if he'd paid attention to the little things while he and Violet were together. Did he reciprocate?

He quizzed himself: Her favorite color was green, and she liked one spoon of sugar and two creams in her coffee. Her best friend was . . . what was her name? Sally or Sandy? Something like that. He'd gotten her a present for her birthday—it'd been a crystal pendant suspended on a fine silver chain. He hadn't ever seen her wear it, except for the night he gave it to her, and now that he thought about it, she didn't often wear silver, favoring yellow-gold rings, earrings, and bracelets. *Nice going, Marsh,* he said to himself.

Standing there loading the dishwasher, he realized he had no idea what she'd done with her days while he was at work. He knew she exercised, went to therapy or some support group intermittently, the house was always spotless, and she read. Though he had no idea what kinds of books. He had always thought she looked cute perched in the bed, her knees drawn up, wearing a pair of his pajama bottoms and wooly socks and black plastic reading glasses, pouring over a book. But had he ever stopped to ask her, "Hey, honey, what are you reading?" He didn't think he had.

Dishwasher loaded, Marshall decided to foray into the bedroom. Maybe it was time he slept in the bed, stretched out, got some decent sleep, instead of cramming his long frame on the sofa, waking up feeling like his body was a length of knotted rope.

The bedroom looked pristine compared to the kitchen and living room. Nothing had been touched since Violet left nearly three weeks ago. He hadn't heard from her, not once. He hadn't tried to call her either since the day after she left, when he called repeatedly, all day long, leaving confused, then hurt, then angry messages on her voice mail. He'd tried email as well, but his messages kept coming back to him as undeliverable. She'd cut him off completely, as if he'd done something unbelievably wrong.

Marshall sat on the bed. The room still felt like their room, even though Violet had taken her things—her books and pictures, the little Victorian lamp her grandmother had given her, her clothes, shoes, and jewelry. The room felt emptier, but still . . . theirs.

Marshall got up and pulled the comforter and bedding from the bed and deposited it in the laundry room. He pulled the mattress and box spring from the bed, hauled them out into the hallway, down the stairs, and out the front door, and left them at the curb outside. He did the same with the bed frame. Once the bed was gone, Marshall took the little rocking chair Violet liked to sit in to read down the hall to the guest room. He rearranged the dressers, then disassembled the bed in the guest room and brought it into the bedroom and put it back together under the big window just the way he'd always wanted it. He liked to open the window a little at night to get some fresh air, which Violet hadn't liked because she got too cold.

Out in the hallway, he dug through the linen closet, and way in the back was the huge brown comforter he'd had in his apartment bedroom when he met Violet. It was nice. He'd picked it out at Ikea in Canton, and though Violet hadn't liked it especially, she'd kept it. Marshall smiled, amazed that something as simple as a blanket could make him feel such . . . relief.

He made up the bed with fresh sheets and his own comforter. He took the framed black-and-white photo of Silver Lake he'd taken when he was twenty-two and the brass lamp from his home office, and he placed the lamp on the nightstand and hung the photo next to the bed. He got the vacuum out and ran it over the carpet, not giving a shit whether or not he woke the downstairs neighbors. Then, exhausted, he took a shower and fell into his new bed and slept like a baby for twelve hours straight.

chapter 14

Tim was full of piss and vinegar. He hadn't answered any of Jennifer's calls while he was out with Costa and the other guys. Six calls, to be exact, and he knew she would be majorly pissed when he got back to Mom and Dad's. The tequila shots he'd done with Costa had washed away the pall of guilt that hung over him like a second skin. He knew Mom and Dad were fine. He made sure they had everything they needed before he left. All Jen had to do was hang out with them, listen to some of Dad's stories she'd already heard fifteen thousand times, and get Mom her pills at 9:00 PM.

Jenny was just mad that he was out and she was stuck with them. Well, fuck her. She'd been no help at all since Tim moved back from Lafayette ten months before. She'd stayed away as much as she could, not helping with anything or giving Tim a break. He knew she was paying him back for leaving. He wished she'd get over it. She'd only taken care of them for a couple of years. Prior to that, it was him constantly checking on them, running them to the hospital. Violet was never much help with that. She said she felt uncomfortable with his parents. He could understand his mom, but Dad always seemed to like her. Like Tim, Jerry Stark was a sucker for a pretty face.

He'd had to bribe Jennifer with a refurbished scanner and fifty bucks to get her to stay with the 'rents while he went out. Even with the bribe, she must have asked him fifteen times what time he was going to be back. He hadn't answered her, so she was pissy before he even left. She started calling at nine thirty. Last text he got was 1:45 AM. It was three twenty now. He hoped she'd just fallen asleep.

He went in through the kitchen door so he wouldn't wake his dad. No such luck on the sleeping sis. Jen was sitting at the kitchen table in the glow of the stove-light. She was sitting cross-legged at the kitchen table glowering at the screen of the portable television. She was watching with the sound off, ticking her fingernails impatiently on the surface of the tabletop. As he'd predicted, she was hot.

"Hey, Jen," Tim said.

"Don't 'hey Jen' me! Fuck you!" she hissed. "Do you know what time it is?"

"Jesus, whose wife are you?" Tim grinned at her.

Jen picked up a banana that had seen better days out of the bowl of fruit on the table and whipped it at him. Tim caught it neatly. It felt squashy. He threw it in the trash bin.

"Give me a break, Jen," he said. "I haven't been out anywhere in weeks."

"Well, now you can see how it feels."

"Oh, don't guilt bullshit me. Mom and Dad didn't need constant care until last year when Dad had the open heart and Mom's legs got so bad. So what'd you have to do? Like two months of it? Stop whining."

"Fuck you, Tim."

"You already said that. Get a new schtick."

Tim reached into the fridge and pulled out a cold bottle of LaBatt's. He twisted the top off and handed it to Jenny, then took another bottle out and opened it for himself. He saw Jenny's expression soften.

"You want to order a pizza?" she said. "I'm starving."

"I left you chicken in the oven." Tim said.

"I'm off chicken." She said. "Ever since that stupid poultry diet."

"But you want pizza?"

"Sure. What's it matter if I'm fat? I'm not going to find anyone anyway."

Tim sighed. He looked at his pretty sister. There were some circles around her eyes that spoke of how exhausted she was, but they were still clear and blue, outlined with a black fringe of lashes. She was slightly on the plump side, but, Tim thought, pleasingly so. Her best feature was her straight, strawberry blond hair that fell shining over one shoulder. "You're not fat, and you will. Why are you in such a hurry, Jen?"

"It's different for women," she said. "Don't you read? You're on the goddamned Internet twenty-four seven. The biological clock. Tick fucking tock."

Tim pulled some cheese out of the refrigerator and some crackers from the cupboard. He set them down on the table in front of his sister. "You're only twenty-six," he said. "Don't rush yourself and end up with someone who's wrong for you. Take my word for it."

"You didn't seem to care about my tender age so much when you took off and left me with Mom and Dad."

Tim hung his head. He didn't want to fight about this again. "Look," he said, sighing. "I'm just saying, don't rush into anything the way I did."

Jen tipped her beer, took a long drink, and belched, something she could do around her brother and her dad. Tim brought a paring knife to the table and started slicing wedges of cheddar. "Yeah," she said. "How'd that go, anyway? Your little Let's Remember Bitchface shindig."

"Shut up, Jen," he said wearily. "Sorry, bro." Jenny stretched, yawning, then raked her hands through her hair, twisted it into a sloppy bun, and wound a hair tie around it. "She was bad news for you, you know."

"True 'nough."

"I was worried about you."

"No shit?"

"No shit," she said.

"It was hard to tell, what with you bitching about Mom and Dad the whole time."

"I wanted to take your mind off your troubles by thinking about mine."

"Ha, ha. How thoughtful of you, sis."

"That's me. Thoughtful." They sat munching on cheese and crackers, the old clock above the stove ticking in the dim kitchen.

"She just dumped her sixth husband," Tim said, washing down a cracker with a swallow of LaBatt's.

"No shit? Another one bites the dust, eh? What's his story?"

"I dunno," Tim said. Suddenly he just didn't feel like talking about it. The whole thing was just . . . weird. "Mom and Dad do okay tonight?" he asked instead.

"Yeah," Jen said. "Mom was on her Publisher's Clearing House tangent again." She punched Tim in the arm. "By the way, what the hell did you do with all her stupid papers? She screamed bloody murder at me about them."

"I threw them out."

Jenny whistled. "Well, bravo for you, but she's pissed."

"She'll forget about it," Tim said, sighing.

"She already did," Jenny said, taking a swallow of her beer. "I distracted her with Rocky Road ice cream. Till tomorrow, anyhow. When she remembers and starts bitching about it, you can deal with it." Jenny got up and pulled her jacket off the back of her chair.

"Hey," Tim said. "It's late. Why don't you stay? You can sleep in my room. I'll bunk on the couch."

"Nah," Jenny said. "I have a class tomorrow at ten. And I want to go for a run in the morning."

"Stay. I'll get up at seven and make you pancakes. Plenty of time to do what you need to do before your class."

Jenny tapped the back of the chair with her fingers. "What kind of pancakes?" she asked.

Tim looked at the bowlful of questionable bananas. "Banana," he said. "With walnuts."

"Are your sheets clean or are there scummy boy germs in them."

"Scummy boy germs," he said.

"Cool." Jen came around the table and kissed him on the top of the head. "I really am glad you're home," she said. "And that you're taking care of things. Mom and Dad, I mean. I'll try to help out more. I know what it's like."

"Thanks." He watched his sister walk down the hall toward his room.

Tim sat thinking about his sister's question. How had the evening gone? Regardless of how nervous he'd felt about going, he'd had a surprisingly good time, despite the negativity that spurred the gathering. They'd all been hurt and abandoned by Violet—and they'd all been charmed by her as well. Tim wondered at that. They all seemed so different from each other.

They all knew about Dead Winston. He'd been a smooth motherfucker. He was older, was business savvy. It'd always been Tim's feeling that Violet had been arm candy for Winston, although to hear Violet tell it, they'd had a "deep, meaningful relationship until his untimely death." It seemed to Tim that Violet had been home a lot while Winston traveled. He brought her expensive gifts, made sure she had everything she ever imagined she wanted, and of course the best therapy money could buy.

Costa was big and booming, outgoing, and generous, and Tim could see a man who was passionate about his family. He might not have a lot of money, but he seemed well enough off. He'd footed the whole bill for dinner and drinking, looking insulted if any of them offered to help pay for anything. He was quick to make a joke and was demonstrative. He'd hugged each of them when they parted, like they were brothers.

In contrast, Brian Jankowicz was quiet and withdrawn. When he spoke, what he said seemed overly thought-out, like he was afraid of making a mistake. He seemed nice enough, but passive. It was hard to imagine Violet with a man like that. Maybe Brian helped her fulfill her motherly instincts. Knowing Violet, though, it was more likely Brian gave her something she needed. She'd holed up with Brian out in the woods and no one had heard from her for a long time. So, she'd most likely been hiding out. It was crazy how Violet could use you and make you feel like she was doing you a favor at the same time.

Marshall and Owen had been harder for Tim to read. Tim understood Marsh's reticence. He hadn't felt like talking to anyone either after Violet left. In fact, he'd been a mess. Marshall seemed to have it together and was the one most instrumental in all of the exes meeting. As the night had worn on, though, he'd gotten quieter and quieter. Tim understood that, too. At the end of the night, Marsh would be returning to a newly empty home. That sucked. Tim knew that firsthand, and he felt for the guy.

Other than that, all he knew about Marsh was that he was a graphic artist, that he did a ton of freelance work, and that he was currently working on some big contract for the city. Tim figured he must do okay from the quality of his clothes and the car he drove, a sexy silver Miata that Marshall seemed worried Violet would try to get in the divorce. She loved driving it, according to Marshall.

Something felt off about Owen, though, and Tim couldn't put his finger on what it was that just didn't sit right with him. He'd laughed, joked, listened. Hadn't shared much though. Maybe he was still broken up about Violet. He had been married to her longer than any of them had—five years. Tim had only been married to her for three years, and he was a mess when they split, was still angry, if he wanted to be honest about it. It seemed to Tim like Owen was holding something back. *Ah, well,* Tim thought. Maybe Owen was just feeling weird about the whole get-together thing. God knew Tim did, too. He finished off his beer, picked up his and Jen's bottles, and put them in the bin by the garage door.

Tim padded into the living room. His dad had fallen asleep with the television on again. He had his feet propped up in the La-Z-Boy, and Jenny must have covered him up with the old afghan his mom crocheted years ago, before her arthritis got so bad. His glasses were askew, and he was snoring softly. It gave Tim a tender feeling, looking at his dad, an older, smaller, softer version of himself, asleep. Tim turned off the television and lay down on the sofa.

He'd slept right here the night Violet left him. He'd been distraught, blindsided by her leaving. Tim had no idea until she left how much he loved her, how much she meant to him. He hadn't known just how deep he'd been in. He worked with computers, software, spent so much time being analytical, that the emotional stuff always surprised him, especially when the emotions were his own.

She told him on a Saturday. She already had her things packed and had done it so neatly and efficiently that Tim hadn't even noticed anything was amiss when he came home from work on Friday night. That night at dinner, Violet had been unusually quiet, but he just thought that maybe she was coming down with something. He thought he'd asked her if she'd felt alright, but he wasn't sure that he'd really done that or if it was a false memory he had, meant to make him feel a little better about himself. He suspected it was the latter.

Tim spent time after dinner online, as he did most nights while Violet cleaned up the dinner dishes. He remembered looking up at one point to see her standing in the doorway of his office staring at him with an expression on her face he was unable to read. "Hey," he'd said.

"Hey," she'd said. "I'm going up to bed. I'm really tired."

"Okay." Tim went back to his computer screen. "Be right up."

But he hadn't been right up. In fact, he didn't go up to bed until 2:00 AM. Violet was asleep. Or at least he thought she was. In the morning over breakfast of coffee and toast, she told him she was leaving. She said she felt unfulfilled, had to find herself, that he was a wonderful man, and she didn't deserve him. She told him she knew how unhappy he'd been and that he was an angel for trying to keep it from her—but a wife just knows, doesn't she?

At first Tim thought she was playing a joke on him. He was

unhappy? How come he hadn't even known? But then again, if anyone had asked him whether he was happy or not, he wasn't sure he would be able to answer. He didn't think about it. He just lived. Day to day. Week to week, like The Doors' song. He'd thought she was kidding, then that she was just doing it to get attention, the way Jenny used to say dramatically as a teenager that she was going to kill herself to get his mother riled up.

Violet told him she wasn't going to change her mind. She told him she already had a place to go, that her things were packed. It was only then that Tim had a good look around and noticed things that were missing. He felt like an idiot.

He told her he wouldn't let her go. They fought. She began to cry, and that was it for Tim. He never could stand the sight of a crying woman, especially Violet. He thought it was best to just let her go. He figured she would stay with a friend for a few days and then she'd call him and they'd talk. He never thought it was permanent. They'd never even had a big fight.

But the divorce papers came right away. She had to have had it planned for a long time, and to add insult to injury, she used money Tim earned to pay the lawyer. He'd wanted to fight it, but Michigan was a no-fault state, his attorney told him. And since they had no children, it was all over in less than thirty days. Tim was devastated. He felt like a failure.

Nothing had ever hit him this hard. He started calling in sick to work, would sit and look at their wedding pictures. He tried calling her, tried to see her, and she refused. She said it was for his own good. Tim cried. A lot. It embarrassed him now to think about it. He couldn't seem to get it together. He stopped seeing friends. He couldn't do his job.

When he got fired from his job with INFOsystems in Flint, he decided to pack it in and leave the state. Jenny'd been pissed because that left her with Mom and Dad. He had to get out. A firm in Indiana offered him a job at less pay than he'd been making, but he took it anyway. He had to be out of Violet's radar. Everywhere he went, it seemed like he could feel her.

Tim lay on the sofa and stared at the ceiling. He wondered how smart it was for the exes to start meeting, talking about what had happened to them. To open the wounds. He wasn't sure. What he did know was, for the first time in a long time, he didn't feel so alone. And that was a good thing. He closed his eyes, listened to the cadence of his father softly snoring, and soon fell asleep.

PROGRESS NOTES: Violet VanDahmm
    CASE NUMBER: V2011-100982
    DATE: 10-20-2011

SUMMARY:

Violet arrived at the appointment flushed and excited. She could barely wait to get started and said she could not wait to talk with me about "Jake." I asked her who Jake was, as during intake she explained that she was separated and single. Violet explained that he is a romantic interest from her past, and that she has "realized" she has been in love with him for years—that this was why she'd been unable to stay in any of the committed relationships she'd pursued thus far. Violet began, at this point, to wax sentimental about "Jake," who she'd had a romantic crush on in high school, more than twenty years ago. Violet stated that she "knows now" what she "really wants," and that she had been trying to locate Jake. She stated that his family has moved from the area, and that calls to high school acquaintances only turned up one lead. She said further investigation on the Internet led her to a business located in Northern Michigan, and that upon calling it, Violet discovered that it is owned by a person of the same name. I asked her if she has spoken to him, and she got a sly look on her face and said it is her plan to surprise him. We discussed the fact that this may not be a good idea, with many years and experiences on both their parts between them. Violet would not be dissuaded, and in fact, she seemed proud that she had "sleuthed" the information on Jake and gotten a hold of an email address for him on her own. Attempts to focus her attention on the fact that she may be choosing to relive the past as a means to avoid current issues (impending divorce, change in the relationship between her and Owen) were met with stubborn silence.

As journal work, Violet was asked to write about her relationship with Jake and why she feels it was an important milestone in her life. Violet stated that she would "try" to work on the journal, but that she had much to do in preparation for seeing "the love of her life" once again.

Yolanda H. Malik, LCSW
Champoor and Associates

chapter 15

Costa let Brian use the phone in the office to call his mom. He sat in the big man's beat-up office chair, his long, ape-like body hunched over, picking at a hole in the knee of his jeans. He pressed the receiver to his ear and listened as the phone rang on his mom's end. It'd been more than three weeks since he'd seen her, and part of him hoped she wouldn't answer.

"Hello," she sounded out of breath.

"Hey, Mom."

"Hubcap?"

"Mom. Don't call me that."

"Well, whatever! Where the hell are you, Brian?" she said. There was a crashing noise on the other end of the line.

"What are you doing?" Brian wanted to put the meat of the conversation off as long as possible. He heard her take a long drag on a cigarette.

"Dishes," his mother said. "Where are you?"

"Saginaw."

"Saginaw! What the hell are you doing there?" His mom's voice got lower. "What part of Saginaw?"

Brian hated it that his family was so bigoted. "The blackest part, Mom," he said, just to spite her.

"Jesus Christ, Hubcap!" she said. "How'd you get there? What are you doing?"

Brian sighed. The hole in his jeans was bigger. Costa wasn't going to like that. He liked the guys in the kitchen to look nice when they were at work, but he hadn't gotten his first paycheck yet. When he did, he was going to get himself some of those workpants like Costa wore in the kitchen. "I got a ride," he said. "And I got a job. And . . . my name is Brian." He gulped. He didn't make a habit out of talking tough to his mom. She was built like a linebacker and was twice as mean.

"Brian? Since when did you care what I called you? What the hell are you doing in Saginaw?"

Brian pulled his fingers away from his jeans. At this rate he was going to be showing off a lot more that a bit of kneecap if he didn't knock it off. Why did she make him so nervous? Brian knew his mom's tough act was just that, an act. She'd had a hard life, especially after his dad left her to raise him and his sister on her own in a ratty town like Omer. He heard her shut the water off, and he imagined her taking a seat at the kitchen table so she could get down to the business of talking sense into her son.

"What the hell, Brian? How are you supposed to get to Saginaw every day to work? What kind of job? What the hell are you thinking? I hope you don't expect me or Charla to drive from Omer all the way to Saginaw. Especially in the winter. Do you see what I am talking about now? This is what happens when you don't take your medication! You can't make a good decision to save your ass!"

"Mom!" Brian was breathing hard. Man, why couldn't she

just give him a chance? He took a deep breath. "Mom," he said a little more calmly. "I am taking my medication. Costa makes me."

"Who's Costa?" she said suspiciously.

"My friend. My boss."

"What kind of name is Costa? Is that his last name? Shouldn't you call him Mr. Costa? You have absolutely no respect for nobody. How do you expect to keep a job if you ain't got no respect?"

"Mom! Jesus! It's his first name. He's Greek."

"Greek?" she said, as if Brian had just told her Costa was a Martian. "From Italy, you mean?"

"From Greece. Or his family's from Greece. I'm working in his restaurant."

"Restaurant?" His mother let out an exasperated sigh. Her voice took on a cajoling tone. "You don't do restaurant work, Hub— I mean, *Brian*. You're a mechanic."

Brian sighed. He thought about his house and his garage and the way he'd been living. He thought about the mail piled up in the mailbox and the calls from bill collectors and angry people who'd needed him to do work for them, people he'd blown off because he couldn't seem to make himself get out of his recliner.

"Well, now I'm learning how to be a cook," Brian said. "A Greek cook."

"What a bunch of bullshit. Who's going to fix my car? Huh?" Brian could hear the *snap snap* of the Zippo and his mother's sharp inhalation as she lit a cigarette. "Well, when are you coming home?"

Brian leaned back in the chair and took a breath to prepare himself. "I'm not coming back there, Mom. Not for a while, anyhow. Maybe to see you, in a few weeks maybe, but not to the house." It was *the* house, not *his* house. It hadn't really felt like a home anyway. Not for a long time.

"A few weeks? What the hell," said his mom. "What are you going to do with the house? Let it rot? You think anyone wants to live in it the way it is? Covered with freakin' hubcaps?"

"I don't know." Brian said. "It's just that, it was me and Violet's house, and I—"

"Violet?" Brian could hear the scraping of a chair and imagined his mother getting to her feet. "Is that what this is about?"

"In a way," said Brian. "Look, Mom—"

"I had enough of her when you were married!" his mother interrupted. "Screwing with your head, thinking she was better than you and everybody else—"

"She didn't, Mom." Brian ran his free hand nervously back and forth through his hair, his mother's voice falling on the back of his neck like a rough hand. He clenched his shoulders up.

"Bullshit! That's history, Hubcap. Over and done with. You're just going to leave your family and a garage full of your daddy's tools to rot while you're off gallivanting in Saginaw with a bunch of who knows whats? You need to go back to that doctor and see what's wrong in that head of yours. You were over it!"

"Really?" Brian raised his voice. "Really, Mom? Over it? I suppose that's why I keep nailing fucking hubcaps to the walls?"

"Don't you fucking swear at me. I'm your mother!"

Brian leaned back in the chair and took a breath. "Look, Mom. I just wanted to know if you or Charla could, you know, please list the house for me. I don't care what I get for it."

"I hope you don't care because you're never going to get a dime for that piece of shit!" his mother said. "What is wrong with your head, Brian?"

"Not as much as there was a couple weeks ago," Brian said. "Look, if you don't want to do it, just say so, I'll figure it out. But if you would, I'd appreciate it."

"I'll do it," his mom said. "I can call Eva Wilson at ReMax, but she's going to laugh her ass off."

"Whatever, Mom." He felt incredibly tired. "Don't sell dad's tools though. I'll come back and clean out the garage. Then you can set it up the way you always wanted with a screen door in the summer and some tables and chairs and stuff, okay?"

"I suppose." His mother took a loud drag on her cigarette. "You're helping me with it, though."

"Sure, Mom."

"Where are you staying?" his mother asked. "Not in some hood, are you?"

"Mom, please," Brian said. "I'm staying with Costa and his wife Angelina and their two kids. For now. Costa's going to help me find a place."

"Why does this Costa person care what happens to you?"

Brian ran a hand through is hair. He sat back in the chair, looking around the cozy office, pictures of smiling children and old people on the walls, and Costa's good chef's coat he kept for special occasions on a hook on the back of the door. Suddenly he felt choked up. He took a deep breath and swallowed it back. "I don't know, Mom," he said. "I don't know."

chapter 16

Owen, Marshall, and Tim sat at the back table waiting for the rest of their group. When Costa came out of the kitchen, Marshall looked at Owen and Tim and said, "Shit. I should have driven up to get Brian."

"No worries," said Costa, smiling, and as if on cue, Brian came out the kitchen door, wearing an apron identical to Costa's.

"Hey," said Brian.

"Hey, yourself," Marshall said. "What's with the get up?"

"I hired him."

"Yeah?" said Owen. "No kidding."

"He's training me." Brian smiled shyly. "It's pretty cool. Even though I never worked in a kitchen before. Only in a garage."

"Hey, that mechanical shit comes in handy, too," Costa said. He leaned across the table. "You know, yesterday, one of my refrigeration units went down, and I am thinking, son of a bitch! Now I godda call the fucking repair guy and he charges a hundred bucks just to answer his phone. Plus parts. So, sonny boy here says lemme look at it, and in twenty minutes he has the bastard working like new." He clapped Brian on the back. "And he fixed the Hobart! Genius!"

Brian's face flushed a deep red. "It was just a bad wire. It wasn't nuthin' to fix."

"Still," Costa said. "You saved me a bundle. Not to mention the food that could have spoiled."

Owen's cell went off, and he pulled it out of his pocket. He looked at the screen and excused himself. "Be right back," he said, hurrying from the table. Tim watched him go. Something was off about that guy. He shook his head and took a drink of his beer. *None of my business,* he thought dismissively.

Out on the sidewalk, Owen hit call-back button. "Hey," he said. "What's up?"

"Hi, Owen." It was Violet.

"Yeah. So, what's going on?"

Violet hesitated. Owen got a premonitory knot in his stomach.

"Are you busy?" she said.

Owen glanced nervously through the glass doors of the restaurant toward the back table. "Well, yeah, I—"

"I made a decision about something today, Owen," she said. "And I really needed to talk to a friend—a male friend about it. And of course, I thought of you first. You're just so . . . level headed."

"I don't know, Violet, I'm kind of—"

"I know, I know. You're a really busy person. And I know our last meeting didn't go very well . . . I'm so sorry about that! But, you see, I just really need someone clear headed to help me out. It's . . . about Jake."

The knot in Owen's stomach clenched. "What about him?" he said tightly.

"Well, I've gotten in touch with him."

"In touch? Like called him? Emailed him? What? I thought you didn't know where he lived."

"I found him. He's living on the other side of the state. I've emailed him."

"So?" Owen was angry. "What do I have to do with it?"

"Why are you acting like this?" she said.

"Like what?"

"Well, kind of jealous," said Violet. "That's kind of silly, don't you think?" She sounded rather pleased at the possibility, further fueling Owen's anger.

"I'm not jealous. I just don't want to talk to you about your high school boyfriend. I heard enough of that when we were married."

"Please, Owen . . . I'm thinking of going to see him."

"So, what do you need to talk to me about, Violet? Sounds to me like you've already made up your mind. As per usual." Owen could feel himself getting wound up. Jake had always been a bone of contention between them. Her high school sweetheart. Her first love. *Blech*. Now, he was making time for her, and she was still going on about him? It was more than a little hard to take.

"Well, I think I'm going to visit him."

"You *think* you are?"

"Well, yes, Owen," she said, an impatience creeping into her voice. "That's why I need to talk to you."

Violet's tone stopped Owen in his tracks. He blew out a breath and ran a hand through his hair. He'd heard that tone plenty of times before, especially toward the end of their marriage. He knew he had to step lightly so that months of subtle wooing wouldn't be for naught. Experience had taught him that the only way to get through to her was to keep his cool, be there for her. Give her what she wanted. He cleared his throat, preparing to give in. Again. "So, when did you want to get together, Violet?"

"Well, I could meet you in half an hour," she said, instantly brightening. "At Tony's on Columbus?"

Owen looked back nervously into the restaurant. He could see the table of men laughing it up. At that moment, Tim looked up and caught his eye. Owen quickly turned away and walked out of Tim's line of sight. "Sure," he said. "I'll be there."

"Thanks," Violet said. "You know, I'm so glad we're friends."

"Yeah," Owen said, frowning. "Me, too."

The guys were still laughing when Owen returned to the table. Tim was holding his stomach. "Good one, Costa," he said, nodding at Owen.

"Goat jokes," said Costa. "Always good for a laugh."

Everyone looked up at Owen. "Everything okay?" Marshall asked when he didn't sit down.

"Yeah, but I . . . um . . . I have to skate," Owen said. "Dog got hit by a car."

"That sucks," said Brian.

"Yeah," Owen said. "You know. Family with kids. Hopefully it's just a case of a broken leg or something."

"Hey, do what you have to do, man," said Marshall. "I'll call you and let you know when and where we're getting together again."

"Cool," said Owen. He fished out his wallet and pulled out a twenty. "But, hey, let me—"

"No. No," said Costa, waving him away. "Get outta here. You didn't even eat."

"Yeah," Tim said. "I have your beer, man. No worries. Go help the pooch."

Owen smiled stiffly and with a nod walked away from the table. Tim watched him go, an odd look on his face.

Marshall looked at Tim. "What?"

Tim watched Owen walk out the door of the restaurant. "I don't know," he said. "It's . . . nothing." But his gut told him something was definitely off.

After the meal and many drinks, the waitress sidled up to the table. "Get you guys another round?"

Tim shook his head. "I have to head out."

Marshall looked at Costa. "One more?" Costa nodded, and the waitress gave them a wink and started to gather up some of the empties. She turned to leave, then stopped, bending down to pick something up off the floor. She came up holding out a cell phone. "This yours?" she asked Tim, who was putting on his coat.

"Looks like Owen's," said Marshall.

"Didn't he say his place was off Mackinaw and Delta?" Tim said. "I have to go right by there." He held out his hand, and the waitress handed him the phone. "I'll drop it off."

"Cool," said Marshall.

Tim gave the guys a nod and dropped Owen's cell phone into his jacket pocket. Maybe, he thought, a little good deed would get the two of them on better footing.

chapter 17

As always, Violet looked fantastic. Her black hair was tousled and sexy, making a perfect frame for her face. She wore a pair of gold hoop earrings that caught the light and an off-the-shoulder sweater in a deep red that accentuated her ivory skin and dark eyes. She waved at Owen from the table. She'd ordered a bottle of merlot, and as he approached, she poured him a glass. She'd forgotten, of course, that Owen hated merlot, and in fact that he preferred any other red wine instead.

"Thanks," he said, sitting down across from her. Tony's was a traditional Italian family restaurant, with red-checkered table-cloths, candles in wine bottles, and family photos on the wall. The waitress brought out a basket of bread and a dish of olives and took their orders.

"Thanks for coming," Violet said.

"I don't know how much help I'll be." Owen shifted in his seat uncomfortably. "You know, I uh . . . I never could stand it when you talked about him."

Violet looked up, fluttering her lashes. She reached over the table and patted his hand. "Well, it's different now. We're friends, not married. But, you know, we should . . . clear the air first," she said.

Oh, no, Owen thought. "Clear the air?" He took a healthy sip of the wine. Merlot or no, it seemed he was going to need it. He grimaced. It tasted especially nasty to him after the top-shelf drinks he'd just had with the men.

"Yes," Violet said. She clasped her hands together like she was going to pray and leaned on her elbows. "Last time we got together, I got the impression you were angry with me—"

Owen opened his mouth to speak, but Violet held up her hand. "No," she said. "Let me finish. I wanted to tell you that . . ." she took a big breath, "you were right."

Owen blinked. He was going to need something stronger than wine. "Excuse me?"

"You were right. I left Marshall because I wasn't happy. Just like I left you and Costa and Tim. And well, poor Brian—that just shouldn't have been. But he's sweet, you know? Helpful." Her eyes got misty. "The only one who ever really left me was Poor Winston."

"He died, Violet," Owen said with an impatient sigh. "He didn't leave you."

She looked down into her lap and said something so quietly that Owen couldn't hear her. He leaned forward. "Excuse me?"

Violet looked up at him, her brows knit together painfully. "I said, he was going to."

"Going to what?"

"Winston was going to leave me," she said. "I . . . I found some paperwork from the attorney after Winston died. Initial paperwork. Questions, you know? How long we'd been married and if either of us were unfaithful and stuff about the money. There was a list of the papers and things the lawyer wanted Winston to get together. For a divorce."

"Wow." Owen sat back. "Why didn't you ever tell me?"

"I didn't tell anybody." Violet looked down into her lap. "Not even Eric, I mean, Dr. Coulter. I didn't want anyone to know. I wondered why the attorney looked at me so funny when he was reading the will."

Owen sat staring at her.

"Oh, don't you get it, Owen?" she said miserably. "Why do you think I am always the one to leave? The one to do the breaking up?" Violet sat back in the booth and folded her arms around her thin frame. "It all stems from the abandonment issues I have from my parents!"

Owen tried not to roll his eyes at the mention of abandonment issues. "Are you saying that's the reason you left me? You thought I'd leave you?"

"Yes," she said, sniffing into her napkin prettily. "You were so unhappy."

Owen pushed his wine away. "I wasn't, Violet! I wasn't unhappy."

The waitress approached the table and placed steaming bowls of soup and salads on the table. Violet pushed hers away. "You were," she said, pouting.

Owen sat, watching her. What good would it do to protest? He thought about the last years of their marriage. His practice had picked up, and he was certainly distracted by that, but unhappy? He didn't think so. He measured unhappiness by how he'd felt in the seven years since the divorce, the unhappiest he'd been in his life. He watched Violet dab at the corner of her eye with her napkin, then look down into her lap. Sometimes being with Violet was like finding yourself dropped into one of those soap operas his mother used to watch every afternoon. Violet could have been one of those sexy soap divas that you love to hate, but looking at her, sitting there like that, softened him.

"You're not going to eat?" Owen said finally. "You didn't eat when we had lunch either."

"I will," said Violet. "I'm just . . . taking a moment to face some things I don't want to face."

For the most part, Owen didn't like seeing her upset this way, but there was a little, hard, mean part deep inside that enjoyed watching Violet squirm. She always seemed so aloof, so above it all, in control. Made it seem like she was doing you a favor while she was crushing your balls in her tiny well-manicured hands. Part of him wanted her to be uncomfortable.

Owen was starving. He hadn't eaten with the guys, and Violet's little confession had heartened him somewhat, even though he'd never admit that to her. He hoped he still had his Concerned Friend look on his face. He *was* concerned about her, but his history with her had also taught him to be concerned about himself as well. He dug into his salad with relish. "So," he said, between bites. "What does Jake have to do with any of this?"

Violet looked at him like he was an idiot. "Well, it's obvious," she said. "Jake was everything I ever wanted!"

Owen put his fork down. "Violet," he said. "Do you have any idea how it makes me feel when you say things like that to me?"

"I don't make you feel anything. *You* feel. No one is responsible for anyone else's feelings."

"I don't want to hear your psychobabble," Owen said. Violet sat back, her eyes going wide.

"If we're going to have a repeat of our luncheon—" she started.

"No, Violet. You're not worming out of it this time. You called me. Not the other way around. And I am doing you a favor. Do you understand? I just lied to my friends and came here to be with you because you said you needed me."

"What friends?"

Owen took up his glass and drained it. *My friends*, he'd said. Were they his friends? Suddenly being here with Violet felt like a betrayal to them. Owen stood up. "Violet," he said. "It doesn't matter. Look, I have to go."

"Owen!" Violet looked confused. "What about Jake? We haven't talked about—"

"I don't give a shit what you do or don't do with Jake." And with that, Owen turned on his heel, leaving Violet to pay the check.

chapter 18

Owen let himself in the house. Bentley was lying in the hall grinning up at him with his fuzzy dog face, smacking his big, uncropped tail on the floor. He'd almost driven back to Costa's after Violet, but he needed some time to process. Plus, he felt like a jerk—both for leaving the guys in the lurch and for his confused emotions about Violet. Owen felt divided. He empathized with Marshall, knew firsthand what the guy was going through. Plus he seemed like a decent enough guy. In fact, all of the exes did, for the most part, and Violet had disposed of each of them as if they were paper towels.

They had other things in common, too: They all seemed to have a sense of humor—you had to if you were in a relationship with Violet. They were pretty steady, had jobs, careers, all of them except Brian—but he had worked steadily as well until Violet left him and he spiraled into his illness. Brian was the youngest of them, and the only one who'd been younger than Violet. His apparent struggle with his illness made him seem even more immature. They were all relatively good-looking guys. Tim was going a little soft in the middle and a little thin on top and Brian was a bit on the scrawny side, but so what?

Owen threw his keys on the stand in the hall and knelt down to scratch Bentley's ears. He'd been well trained to not jump up on Owen when he came home at night. Bentley rolled over on his back for a belly scratch. "What do you think, boy?" he said. "Wanna go for a walk?" It was a beautiful autumn evening, the smells of summer fading into the heady aroma of fallen leaves. Walking was a good way, Owen thought, to clear his muddled mind.

The mutt was up in a flash, wiggling and wagging his massive tail. Owen grabbed the leash from the hall table and snapped it on. "Come on, buddy," he said, opening the front door. Bentley's ears immediately pricked up, and he stood staring out the door at attention. Owen turned to see what had upset the canine and was surprised to see Violet's Saab parked by the curb.

"Shit," he muttered to himself.

When Violet saw Owen, she opened the door and climbed out, flashing a shapely leg Owen couldn't help staring at. "He's cute," she said as the pair approached her car. "What's his name?" She held her hands out to pet him, and Bentley the Traitor went right to her.

"Bentley," Owen told her.

Violet bent down and rubbed the dog's ears. "Oooh," she said. "Aren't you a good boy?" Bentley wiggled his butt in the affirmative. "I can't believe you finally got a dog."

"What are you doing here?" said Owen.

"Being a friend. A real one."

"What's that supposed to mean?"

"What's going on with you, Owen?" Violet leaned back against her car, her arms folded across her chest. She looked beautiful, standing there with the streetlights cascading down on her witchy hair, her skin white as milk. Owen wanted to reach out and stroke her cheek, and a memory came unbidden, a flash of them walking along the beach in the Keys with the moon falling on her then just like the streetlight was now, the way he'd taken her in his arms and kissed her. They'd made love on the beach that night.

Owen looked at her and swallowed. "What do you mean, what's going on with me?"

"Why so defensive, for one thing?" That know-it-all voice irritated him so badly.

"I don't know what you're talking about, Violet," he said. Bentley was doing the pee-pee dance, his big tongue lopping out of his mouth. He looked up at the two of them, his eyes begging. "Look, I have to walk him or he's going to urinate all over my shoes. Or yours." Bentley was rubbing against Violet, begging for another pat.

She peeled herself away from the car. "So, let's walk."

Owen shook his head. He'd really wanted some solitude. He hated it when Violet was pushy like this—and hated it even more that he always gave in to her. He turned and started walking, Violet stepping in beside him. Her heels went *click-click-click* on the pavement, matching time with the *scritch-scratching* of Bentley's nails. It was like walking with a percussion section.

They walked to the end of the block before either of them spoke. For Owen, it felt a little surreal, walking like this with her, the way they used to at night after dinner, saying hello to neighbors like a normal married couple, looking at the stars over the tops of the oaks and birch and pines. It didn't feel normal now. Now they were walking with the ghost of what they used to be, and it made Owen's already jumbled thoughts even more confused. He reached down and scratched Bentley's ears, glad to have his furry friend walking beside him.

Violet's voice was a gentle breeze in the night. "You've been different with me ever since I told you about me and Marshall."

"You never really told me about you and Marshall. You told me about you." Owen kept his attention focused on the sidewalk ahead of him. He didn't want to look at her in this light. He wanted to hang on to his resentment a little.

"Why so angry, Owen?" She walked ahead of him a little and spun around. She had her arms clasped around herself, as if she were cold. "I thought you'd be happy we were splitting up."

Owen stopped and faced her. "What's that supposed to mean?"

"I'm not stupid, Owen." She looked into his eyes.

He turned away and continued walking quickly down the sidewalk and turned the corner. He heard her scurrying behind him to catch up. As he started up the block, Violet caught up to him. She touched him on the arm, and he stopped, Bentley sitting on the sidewalk between them, thumping his tail.

"Look, I know you have feelings for me," she said.

"If you know that, Violet," he said, "why the hell are you asking me to talk to you about Jake?"

"Because you're smart," she said. "And you know me. And you know about Jake. And you're sensible." Violet looked down at her shoes. "I'm tired of making mistakes."

"I'm tired of being thought of as a mistake," said Owen irritably. "I have to take Bentley home and feed him." He started walking.

"That's not what I meant, Owen."

"Then learn to say what you mean." Owen kept walking away from her. He let Bentley run, and he jogged after him, leaving Violet in the dark.

chapter 19

On the passenger seat, Owen's phone lit up and began to play The Bangles' "Eternal Flame." Tim reached over and turned down the Rolling Stones and grinned as the phone trilled out the melody again. He chuckled a little at the vet's choice of ringtones and looked at the lit screen. Instead of a call, it was a text message coming in. Tim did a double take, staring at the phone, glancing up just in time to see his Jeep meandering toward a fire hydrant. His foot hit the brake and the Jeep screeched to a stop, file folders and fast food wrappers flying off the seat onto the floor. On the screen, the name VIOLET was lit up in bright purple text. "Holy shit," Tim said aloud. He pulled the Jeep over to the curb.

Tim sat staring at the phone, his thumb poised on the message button. He was dying to see what it said but knew Owen would be able to tell he'd read the message. He threw the phone down as if it were a hot potato and sat, looking out the windshield. He'd known something was off about the guy, and Tim couldn't help wanting to know what it was. His gut had even told him something was hinky about the dog story—what if there wasn't even a pooch? What if Owen had made it up? What if it had been Violet who'd called him at the restaurant? *Not cool,* Tim thought, *not cool at all.* On the seat, the phone lit with Eternal Flame again. Tim reached over quickly and shut it off. He was going to go over there right now and find out from Owen what the hell was going on.

There was a Volvo parked on the tree-lined street in front of Owen's house. A woman was in the shadows leaning against the passenger door of the Volvo, talking to a man. There was something familiar about them, and instinct made Tim pull over and park, killing the lights on the Jeep. Tim squinted into the darkness. The woman took a step toward the man, and he stepped back, throwing up his hands and drawing both of them out into the arc of the streetlights. He had a dog on a leash, and the dog danced around excitedly. Tim leaned forward in his seat, his breath fogging the windshield. It was definitely Violet and Owen.

Tim couldn't believe what he was seeing. It was the first time he'd gotten a glimpse of his ex-wife since they'd divorced. His heart hammered in his chest. On the street, Violet reached out and put her hand on Owen's arm. Owen started walking, and Violet followed him. Even from where he was sitting, Tim could see her jabbering at him. It was like watching a movie, the drama queen running to catch her quarry. The couple turned the corner, disappearing behind the house.

Tim turned on the lights and pulled out, inching ahead. He looked around the corner. They'd stopped to talk again, then Owen jogged away, on the heels of the pooch (so there was a pooch after all, but not a half-dead one), leaving Violet standing under a streetlight. She watched Owen moving away from her, then turned to walk back the way they'd come. Tim sped away, not wanting to be seen.

He fished his cell phone out of his pocket and scrolled down to Marshall's number. He was about to hit dial when he stopped. Why call Marsh and get him all riled up? Tim knew what he'd do, and it would serve the little prick right for lying to them. He'd wait until they met again and out him to everyone. Owen could suffer the wrath of the whole group. Tim angrily turned up the Stones and headed home.

At home, Tim sat in the driveway, thinking. Part of him felt like a dick, spying the way he had. He hadn't meant to, he really had intended to just take Owen his phone, maybe dispel a little some of the suspicion he felt in his own gut. And now Owen's cell phone was still lying on the passenger seat. Tim scooped it up and put it in his jacket pocket. He was going to have to figure out how to get it back to Owen. He thought about what he'd seen, the way Violet had looked under the streetlights. She was still beautiful. It made Tim's heart lurch in a way he didn't like or understand. He liked to think he was over all that. It's what he told people, after all. But if he was over it, he thought, why would he have agreed to meet with the other exes in the first place?

His reverie was broken by the sight of the porch light blinking on and off. He looked up to see Jenny's oval face in the kitchen window. Tim grinned, remembering how their dad used to blink the porch lights like that when Jenny's dates used to bring her home, and how mad it used to make her. He climbed out of the Jeep and headed into the house.

"What the hell were you doing out there?" she said, sliding into her coat.

"Thinking." Tim threw his keys on the counter.

"Yeah, I think I smell some scorched brain cells."

"Har har," Tim said, taking a playful swat at his sister.

Jenny threw her purse strap over her shoulder. "Gotta go."

"Everything okay with Mom and Dad?"

Jenny rolled her eyes at him. "Everything's the same," she said, and she went out the door. Tim checked on his mom, poking his head in her bedroom doorway from the hall. As he shut her door softly, he heard his sister come back in the kitchen door. As he appeared in the doorway of the kitchen, Jenny threw her bag on the table with a thud. "Son of a bitch!" she said.

"What's up?"

"Stupid car's dead in the driveway again."

"Gimme a minute," Tim said. "I'll go take a look. Maybe it just needs a jump. I have cables in the Jeep."

He shrugged his coat back on and went out. He popped the hood on Jenny's '89 Oldsmobile. The damn thing was on its last legs. Tim wished he made more money. He'd help his sister with a decent car. She was trying so hard with school and all. Jenny came out and sat behind the wheel, trying to get the car to turn over while Tim tinkered under the hood. He had no idea what he was doing. Computers, routers, and networks, yes; car engines, no. Most IT guys he knew were the same way. He hauled his jumper cables out and hooked them up but had little faith that it would do the trick. He started his Jeep and let it idle a bit, then stuck his head out the window. "Give it a try!"

Instead of hearing her car turn over, he heard Jenny swearing like a sailor. They got out of their cars, and Tim unhooked the cables. Jenny sat in her dead car, her hair hanging in her face. She looked like a lost kitten.

"Now what am I supposed to do? I have school and work tomorrow."

Tim took out his key ring. He fished off the key for his Jeep.

"Here," he said. "I'll make do. I have plenty of work here and no deliveries tomorrow. Just bring it back tomorrow night when you get out of class."

"What am I supposed to do about my car?"

"I know someone," Tim said.

"You know someone." Jenny looked at him suspiciously. "I don't want you and your computer geek buddies goofing with it. It's in bad enough shape already. Since when do you know someone?"

"There's this guy I just met," Tim said. Jenny opened her mouth to protest. "A mechanic. For real," Tim insisted.

"A real mechanic?"

"Yeah."

"How much?"

"How do I know? I don't even know what's wrong with the fucking piece of shit," Tim said. "Look, don't worry about it. I'll work it out."

"What do you mean, work it out?"

"I'll pay for it," he said, steering his sister toward his Jeep. "As a favor for you helping me out lately. I appreciate it."

He opened the door for her, and she climbed in. "I have to say you've been in a better mood," she said.

"Really?" Tim leaned on the doorframe and thought about his anger over Owen and Violet. Perhaps Jenny had been seeing even a tougher side of him most of the time. She fired up the ignition.

"Yeah," said Jen, punching him in the arm. "You're not quite as much of an asshole as usual." She smiled. "So, are you guys going out and getting laid or what?"

"No."

Jenny laughed. "Might do you some good." She looked at her brother's pensive face. "What?"

Tim looked up at her. "Nothing."

"Seriously, what? What's with the look? Something happen?"

Tim thought again about Owen and Violet standing together under the umbrella of trees. He gave his sister a half smile. "It's all good," he said. "Go home."

"Going," she said, grinning. "See you, bro."

chapter 20

Marshall and Costa sat at the table finishing off a bottle of Tsaoussi. Brian was in the kitchen helping Niki with the last of the closing chores, and one of the girls was vacuuming up front. Costa had his feet propped up on a chair next to him, and Marshall was lounging across the banquette.

"It's nice what you're doing for Brian," Marshall said.

"He's a good kid." Costa'd never had a little brother, only sisters, but he imagined if he'd had a brother, and that brother was in need, he'd help him much the same way he was helping Brian. All the kid needed was a little push, a little guidance, like Costa'd gotten from his father, his brothers, and uncles. It was a shame Brian's dad had run out on them when he was a boy.

Marshall took a drink of the sweet, fruity wine. He leaned his head back against the banquette, savoring it. "I never thought of myself as much of a wine drinker," he said, "But this is fucking good."

Costa nodded. "From Greece. My dad knows someone on the island of Cephalonia."

"You really are a decent guy," Marshall said. "I'm sorry I thought you and Violet—"

Costa held up his hand. "No worries. Is past. And hey, we all had our doubts about Violet at one time or another, huh?" He took a drink of his wine. "She was like . . . what's that weird metal liquid?"

"Mercury?"

"Yeah. Didn't they used to call it quicksilver?"

Marshall nodded.

"Yeah, that," Costa said.

"You're kind of a poet," Marshall said, smiling.

"Hey, I'm Greek. It's in the blood."

"Do you think this is stupid? All of us getting together like this?"

Marshall looked at Costa, and the older man could see the weariness in the younger man's face. He was having a harder time than he'd admit, but all in all, he was sure holding it together better than Costa had when he was in the same boat.

"The guys?" Costa said. "Nah. It's good. Hey," he said. "We're like brothers."

"We did sorta gel right away, didn't we?"

"Common ground," said Costa. They sat in silence for a moment. Then Costa leaned forward and lowered his voice. "So, how you really doing, huh?"

Marshall let out a sigh. "I don't know. I haven't heard from her. I expect next time I do it will be in divorce court. I wonder about the house. If she'll want it. There's still some of her stuff there."

"She won't," said Costa, shaking his head. "Violet doesn't like to go back to the scene of the crime."

"Yeah," said Marshall. "I'm not sure I want to stay there either."

"I know what you mean," Costa said.

Marshall laughed. "I threw the bed out."

"No shit?"

"Right out on the curb. After our first meeting with the guys. It was only out there like twenty minutes. Some one in a beat-up truck stopped and took it."

"Don't rush yourself." Costa poured the last of the wine in their glasses. "But don't stay in a rut either."

"What kind of fucked-up advice is that?"

"You godda listen to your heart." Costa downed his drink, then started stacking the empty glasses and dishes.

"Christ," Marshall said. "Am I going to start hearing violins in a minute or what?"

"Don't be a prick. What I'm saying is, give yourself some time to get your feet on the ground, and be careful with yourself—you know what I mean by that. You don't want to end up in a shit hole like I did. But don't close yourself up either. That's why this thing with the guys is good. Keeps you from doing that—and hey, we get to work some stuff out, too."

"You have things pretty worked out, seems to me," Marshall said.

"You move on," Costa said. "And I was lucky. I got Angelina. But, you know, yourself as a younger man, when you look back it's like you're looking back at a younger brother—do you know what I mean?"

Marshall nodded, although he wasn't sure he was exactly following.

"Like it's yourself, but not yourself," Costa explained. "Because you would never make the same mistakes now . . ." he looked Marshall dead in the eye, "or at least you hope that you wouldn't. But you are still connected to that younger man. You understand him, why he did the things he did, felt the things he felt."

"You're talking about regrets." Marshall thought about the

photo of Violet he'd jammed into the desk drawer, her wedding ring, still lying near the kitchen sink. During his late-night purging, that was the one thing he hadn't been able to touch.

"Okay. Regrets." Costa held up the empty bottle of Tsaoussi. "So, sometimes, I drink too much wine—but it's good wine—and get thinking about things, and I have regrets. Violet wasn't always a prize, but I had my moments, too. What do they say, takes two to tango." Costa stood up. The vacuum had gone quiet, as had the banging in the kitchen. "I godda get this place closed up."

Marshall finished his wine and stood, extending his hand. Costa took it and gave him a solid shake. "Thanks again," Marshall said.

"You bet."

Outside, Marshall stood on the sidewalk, breathing in the cool air. Above him a million stars winked beyond the haze of the city's lights and light smog. He wondered how long it would be before he heard from Violet, or her attorney, more likely. He thought of Costa's words: Don't rush, but don't stay in a rut either. Marshall was sleeping better since he rearranged the bedroom. He'd consider that his victory for now.

chapter 21

Tim called Jenny in the afternoon. "Hey," he said, "my guy's here. We have to go get some parts for your car. How soon can you be here?"

"I'm actually on my way over. I just finished work," she said. "But I have class in a couple of hours."

"Brian says he can have this fixed for you in about an hour, if you can hang here with Mom and Dad for a little while so we can get the stuff he needs at the auto parts store."

"Who's Brian?"

"My guy. Are you coming?"

"Where'd you meet him?"

"Jen. For Christ sake."

"Is he cute?"

Tim sighed impatiently. "Are you coming over here or not?"

"Yes, yes," Jen said. "I'll just bring my homework there. Big test next week. I'm getting close to my clinicals."

"Yeah?" He wanted to tell her he was proud of her, but his brotherly stubbornness held him in check. He smiled anyway. Why was he so hard on the kid? She was a good egg.

"Been working my butt off."

"I know you have." He paused, then said quietly, "Hey, Jen, you know I'm proud of you, right?"

"Yeah," she said. "Shut up. You're creeping me out." Tim grinned, imagining her smiling at the other end of the line.

When she came in the back door a few minutes later, Tim was inside getting Brian and himself a couple of sodas.

"Where'd you meet him?" Jenny said, peering out the window toward the driveway, where Brian was looking under the hood. "He's kinda cute."

"At the sup— the guys I've been hanging with," Tim said.

Jenny started laughing. "Oh! That's great! You mean your group of Violet freaks? Wait a minute." Jenny grabbed Tim by the arm. "You don't mean, he . . . ?" She aimed a thumb at the driveway.

"Yeah," Tim said. "Him, too."

"No fucking way."

"Nice mouth on you, Nurse Ratched."

"Come on. You're pulling my leg." Jenny grabbed one of the sodas Tim had just opened off the counter and took a big slurp out of it. Tim shook his head and turned to the refrigerator for another. "He was married to Violet?"

"Yeah," Tim said. "For a little while."

"Shit. So were you—for a *little* while." Jenny went to kitchen door and looked out again at Brian through the window. "Nah. He's too cute to have been married to Violet."

"Thanks, sis."

"No, really." Jenny kept staring out the window, chewing on

her thumb. "He's young. Younger than you, anyhow." She looked at her brother. "And he *is* cute."

"Yeah, he's peachy."

"Does he have a girlfriend?"

"Don't you think that would be a little weird, Jen?"

"What?"

"Dating some guy that used to be married to your ex-sister-in-law?"

Jenny brightened. "You think he'd date me?"

Tim sighed. That's what he got for wishing Jenny would meet someone. At least Brian seemed like a nice guy—even though he was a little screwed up. But he was a far cry from the kinds of guys Jenny used to date—the lazy, self-involved ones that broke her heart. "I have to go back outside." He elbowed Jenny out of the way and went out the door.

"Hey," she called.

Tim turned back.

"Hey, what?"

"What's wrong with my car?"

"Bad starter. Had to get a new one."

"How much?"

"Don't worry about it." Tim walked away and joined Brian. He set a soda can on the engine block.

"Thanks," Brian said, pulling the bad part out and setting it on the ground at Tim's feet. "Recycle pile."

Tim stood there, gawking. "Don't have a recycle pile."

Brian picked up the soda. "Just start one in the garage. Metal and stuff, and when I take a ride back to Omer, I'll put it with the rest of the scrap metal. You can make some money with scrap, you know."

Tim thought about how he'd considered an IT recycling

business, but without more room or a place of his own, it just hadn't been feasible. Tim thought it might be a good idea to talk with Brian about that sometime.

They leaned against the car and drank. After a moment Brian said, "So, that was your sister, huh?"

"Yeah," Tim said. "Jenny."

"Hm," Brian said noncommittally.

"She's going to school to be a nurse."

"She's kinda cute," Brian said, his face flushing a deep pink.

Tim smiled at his new friend. "Really," he said, chuckling. He glanced toward the kitchen window and caught Jenny peeking out at them. She ducked away when she saw him looking. "Well, how about that."

PROGRESS NOTES: Violet VanDahmm
    CASE NUMBER: V2011-100982
    DATE: 11-03-2011

SUMMARY:

Violet arrived somewhat agitated and was not as carefully put together as she'd been at previous appointments. She stated that she'd taken the day off work to "get herself together." When asked what was distressing her, she said she was confused and upset, that "Jake" was ignoring her and that Owen was "being mean" to her.

I told her it was my observation that Owen's opinion of her seemed to matter to her a great deal. Also that she spoke of him as having residual feelings for her—was it possible she has some for him as well? Violet vehemently denied having any feelings beyond those of "friendship" and "maybe even feeling a little sorry for him." When asked why she felt sorry for Owen, Violet refused to answer and said that while his "recent attitude toward her" bothered her, she was more upset about Jake.

When asked how she was feeling about her divorce, Violet became tearful and said she had not heard from Marshall. I asked her whether she'd expected to, given the circumstances, and she shrugged noncommittally then replied, "I suppose." I asked her how she felt about not hearing from him, to which she responded, "Kind of bad." She identified that she felt sorry about "Marshall's unhappiness" but stated that he had not talked about being unhappy, but that she "knew" it was how he felt. Violet seemed to become increasingly restless during the conversation, twisting her hands in her lap and sitting on the edge of the seat. When asked about this, her demeanor suddenly changed. She began talking about her anticipation of her "new life" and "new love" with Jake, even if he wasn't responding as eagerly as she had hoped. She explained that she can now clearly see what she really wants, and that she will do whatever she can to attain it.

I suggested that with the passage of time, many things change in people's lives and that she could look at her own life as an example—what if Jake has married or is involved in a serious relationship? Violet became agitated and stated she does not want to think about that, and that the "universe" would "just not allow that to happen." She stated that she and Jake were "soul mates." She stated that when he responds to her email message, she will plan a visit to surprise him. I told her that I have several concerns regarding this idea. Violet states that she will "be wonderful" once she is reunited with Jake.

It is obvious there are several issues this client could be working on. I made a suggestion that we meet once per week for a while. Violet said she will think about it, but she did not feel it is necessary.

We discussed Violet's lack of personal work in her journal. Violet made a commitment to work on this for the next session, stating, "I'll have a lot to write about!"

Yolanda H. Malik, LCSW
Champoor and Associates

chapter 22

Marshall watched the pretty young woman walk back to her car. He wondered if she thought he was a chump. *What a crappy job*, he thought, *serving people divorce papers.* He stood on the porch with the envelope in his hands, the rainy autumn day perfectly matching his mood. He gazed at the cold, technical language that gave Violet the power to end their marriage. He knew there was no use trying to fight it. This was happening to him. He never thought this would happen to him. He remembered his parents fighting when he was a kid, how he'd felt, listening to the bickering, the bitter comments afterward by both his parents. He swore it would never be like that for him, and now here he was.

He stayed there for a long time, the damp and cold penetrating his socks. He stared at the houses across the street. Dusk was falling, and some of the houses had lights on inside, looking warm and cozy. Marshall imagined people getting ready to eat dinner together, kids finishing homework. Families. Though he'd known Violet couldn't have children, he'd been planning to talk to her about adopting a child. He'd just wanted the business to be more lucrative, so he'd put the conversation off a month, two months, a year. Maybe adopting a child would have changed things between them. He chided himself for waiting too long.

The frigid air seeped in through his clothes, and he shivered, yet he remained. Costa talked about regret, and that was something Marshall had in spades. He missed simple things, like Violet's compact little body curved in a crescent on the other side of the bed, listening to her soft breathing in the night, coffee at the kitchen table on Sundays with the *Detroit News* spread out between them, even her silly, frilly underwear that she always carefully washed by hand hanging on the shower rod. Marshall turned and went back in the house. His hands and feet were numb. October had turned suddenly chilly, and he wondered if tonight it would frost.

Marshall sat down at the kitchen table with the sheaf of papers, reading them carefully, though they really said nothing personal. It was just a bunch of legal gobbledygook. He could choose to "file an answer," which in his estimation would only postpone the inevitable. By law in Michigan, he couldn't fight the divorce. Either way you cut it, if it was what Violet wanted, it was going to happen. He had twenty-one days to respond. He ran a hand through his hair. What good would waiting do? *Absolutely none*, he thought to himself. He stood abruptly and stalked to the desk. He grabbed a pen and signed his name quickly on all the copies, then sealed them in the self-addressed envelope that had been provided. Before he could change his mind, he put a stamp on the envelope, slid into his shoes and coat, and headed out the door to the nearest mailbox.

As Marshall slid the envelope through the slot, hearing it drop with a soft *whoosh* into the bottom, a dull ache settled in his gut.

He walked eleven blocks to the nearest liquor store and bought a pint of bourbon, hoping it would take the edge off the chill he felt in his chest.

chapter 23

The guys decided to meet at Barney's Pub on Braddock. The old bar had been owned by the Dell family since it opened in the 1920s, and it still had a reputation as a men's hangout—usually mostly empty with a couple of old regulars at the bar. They met up at eight o'clock, giving Costa and Brian a chance to help Niki get over the worst of the dinner rush before sneaking out. It had gotten cold, the temperature dropping to the 30s, and soon the evening streets would be filled with little kids in costumes raiding their neighbors for treats.

Costa ordered a round of Jelly Beans as soon as he was through the door. The waitress came to the table with the licorice-flavored shots on a round tray.

"What ya celebrating?" she asked.

Tim thumbed in Marshall's direction. "Divorce," he said.

The waitress winked at Marsh. "What doesn't kill ya' makes ya' stronger." She leaned over to deposit the drinks, giving Marshall a nice show of her ample cleavage. "My gramma told me that."

"Smart woman," Costa said. "Light 'em up."

The waitress produced a lighter from her pocket and set the shots aflame. "Cheers, boys," she said, walking away with a definite swing in her back yard.

Costa picked up his drink. "To Marshall," he said, blowing out the flame and downing the drink. "Opa!"

"Opa!" the others cheered, putting back the shots.

"Damn!" Owen said, grimacing. "That's nasty!" He slid the shot glass across the table and reached for his drink.

"Pussy," said Costa.

"Fuck you," Owen said, good-naturedly.

"Enough for me," said Brian. He picked up his Coke and washed the taste of the anise liquor away. "Really not supposed to drink . . . with my meds and stuff." He colored a bit.

"How are you doing?" Marshall asked him. "With your meds and stuff."

"He's doing quite fine, if you ask me," Tim said, a shit-eating grin on his face.

"Shut up," Brian blushed a deeper shade of pink.

Marshall looked from Tim to Brian and back again. "What's going on?" he asked.

Brian looked down into his lap, hiding an embarrassed grin. "Nothing."

Costa patted him on the back. "He's a gentleman. No kissing and telling, eh?"

"Kissing and telling?" Marshall sat up a little taller in his seat and leaned forward. "Do tell."

"No shit?" Owen chimed in. "You went on a date?"

"He did," said Tim, grinning. "Few nights ago. With my sister, Jenny."

"No shit!" Marshall said, clapping Brian on the back. "Cool, man."

"It's nothing," said Brian. "We just went to dinner. At Costa's." He looked at the older man for support.

"Hey," Costa said. "Dinner at Costa's. Sounds like a big deal to me. Romantic."

Brian looked at Tim. "She's nice," he said. "Really nice."

"Yeah," Tim said, looking like the proud papa. "She's a good kid."

"Just take it slow," said Costa.

"We just met!" Brian's face looked like a pickled beet.

"Well, good for you," said Marshall. He leaned back in his chair. "So, I'm officially getting divorced. Brian, here, went on a date. What else is happening?"

Tim leaned forward. The men looked at one another. It was the moment he'd been waiting for. Marshall raised an eyebrow at him. "What's up with you?"

Tim shifted uncomfortably in his chair. He shrugged a little and took a drink of his beer, looking at Owen over the rim of his glass. Owen was looking down into his drink. He looked up, catching Tim staring at him.

"What?" Owen said.

"Well, you've got some news, don't you?" he looked meaningfully at the Owen.

"What are you talking about?" Owen got a sudden bad feeling in his stomach. Tim had been looking at him weird ever since he'd arrived, and Owen wondered what was up. It looked like he was going to find out, and he had a pretty good idea he wasn't going to like it.

"Well," Tim said, drawing the moment out. "You've got a lady in your life as well." He looked Owen directly in the eye, challenging him. "Don't you?"

"I don't know what you mean," Owen said tightly.

The tension at the table was suddenly thick. "What's going on?" Marshall said, he and Costa and Brian looking at each other. Costa shrugged.

"Yeah, Owen," added Tim. "Why don't you tell the guys what's going on. I think Marshall would be particularly interested in hearing about your little girlfriend."

Owen's face got pale. "Son of a bitch," he said under his breath.

Marshall looked at Tim. "What are you talking about?" he asked.

Tim kept his eyes on Owen. "Well," he said. "Guess who lied to us about his doggy emergency the other night so he could meet up with a woman?"

The men at the table let out a collective breath. Marshall looked over at Tim. "Hey, I'd throw this pack of ugly mugs over for a woman any day," Marshall said. He turned to Owen. "Well, it's cool. You could have told us, though. When did you meet her?"

"It's Violet," Tim said. There was dead silence at the table as everyone turned to Owen. Suddenly, Marshall was up like a shot. He was breathing shallowly, not taking his eyes off Owen. "It was you," he breathed. "I thought it was Costa, but it was you." He lunged across the table. Owen wasn't fast enough. Marshall grabbed him by the collar and punched him in the face, and Owen went down in his chair, clutching his jaw. Marshall slipped around the table, yanking him up. Owen ineffectually slapped at Marshall, who took another swing and missed. The men got each other in a head lock, going round and round clumsily, knocking over chairs.

Costa looked at the two men thrashing at each other. He turned to Brian as he got out of his chair, pushing up his sleeves. "They fight like girls," he said. "I'll take the hot head and you take the doc." Brian nodded at Costa and scooted around the table toward Owen.

"Hey!" shouted the waitress. She looked at the old geezers sitting at the bar, making a point of ignoring the scene, and threw up her hands impatiently and ran over to the table herself. "Knock it off! I'm calling the police."

"You fucker!" Marshall yelled, grabbing Owen's shirt, popping off the top buttons. They danced across the surface of the table and skittered to the floor. "You were fucking my wife!"

"No I wasn't!" Owen squeaked. "You've got it all wrong."

Tim sat back, drinking his beer and enjoying the show. Costa shot him a look. *Asshole*, the look said. Tim just shrugged and took a long swallow of his beer.

"Come on, sonny boy," Costa grabbed a flailing Marshall. "You wanna end up in jail?" Brian squeezed in and nabbed Owen. The men were breathing heavily, sweating and red-faced.

"Come on. Come on." Costa pushed Marshall down into his chair. The waitress gave them all a dirty look and skulked back to the bar.

"It was him!" Marshall said, narrowing his eyes at Owen.

"It's not what you think!" Owen hissed. He looked over at Tim, lowering his voice to a hiss. "How the fuck did you find out?" Tim shrugged smugly and took Owen's cell phone out of his pocket. He slid it across the table. Owen wiped blood from his mouth. "You stole my phone?"

"You dropped your phone. I was on my way to return it, and I saw the two of you together. What do you have to say about that?"

Owen took a step toward Tim, but Brian was standing at the ready. He put a hand on Owen's chest. Costa stood with his grip on Marshall's shoulder. "We're friends," said Owen, backing down. "That's all."

"Friends?" said Tim and Brian at the same time.

"Fuck you," Marshall said.

"Are you done?" the waitress called, her arms folded across her chest.

"We're good," Costa patted Marshall roughly on the back. "Bring us another round, okay, sweetheart?"

"Are you going to fuck up my bar anymore?"

"No," Costa said. "All under control." He looked from Marshall to Owen. "Right, boys?"

"We're good," Owen said.

"Fuck you," Marshall said again, looking away. The men all sat back in their places. Marshall glowered.

Costa leaned toward Tim. "What the fuck's wrong with you?"

Tim looked at Costa incredulously. "What the fuck's wrong with me?" He set his empty glass on the table. "What about vet boy here? He violated the code, man."

"Code? What code?" Costa wanted to know.

"Bros before hoes."

Brian reached over and grabbed Tim by the arm. "Shut up, man," he said.

"What?"

"Just stop it."

"You think this guy violated a code? Like brotherhood?" Costa said. "What about what you just did?"

"He was uncovering this fucker's lies," Marshall said, nodding at Owen.

"Exactly," said Tim.

"Bullshit," said Costa.

"I saw them together." Tim leaned forward and pointed at Owen. "Tell them!"

"What are you talking about?" Owen asked.

"Taking a little romantic stroll instead of supposedly going to save a dog's life for some poor family?" Tim said. "Jesus, dogs and kids? How low are you?"

Owen took a deep breath. He looked at Marshall. "Look," he said. "I'm . . . sorry, man."

"You're sorry?" Marshall shook his head.

"Really, just friends," Owen said. "We've been friends, if you want to call it that, since she and Tim split up." Tim looked down in his lap and shook his head.

"Wait a minute," Marshall said. "You were seeing each other the whole time we were married?"

"She invited me to your wedding," Owen said.

"Shit," said Costa.

"Why didn't she tell me?" Marshall said.

Owen pointed to his bloody mouth.

"Point taken," said Marshall.

"This is fucked up," Tim said. "Here, we're meeting because we were all married to her, all affected by what she did to us, and the whole time, you're talking to her? Isn't that a breach of . . ." He looked to the other men for support, and all he got in response were a bunch of hardened, blank looks. "Well, it has to be a breach of something."

"Does seem kind of shitty," Marshall agreed. He rubbed at his knuckle, then looked at Costa. "I told you this was a dumb idea." Costa looked away and put up a finger, signaling the waitress for another shot.

The waitress came over to Costa and said, "Look, you seem to kinda be in charge here. So, I'm telling you things need to stay calm. You feel me? She looked at the men meaningfully. "And understanding that working women deserve really big tips."

"Of course," Costa winked at her and handed her a wad of bills.

Marshall looked at Owen. "You're friends with Violet?" he asked.

"That's what she calls it," Owen said. There was a round of knowing nods from the other men.

"Why you?" Marshall said. "And none of these other guys?"

"I don't know," Owen said. "Maybe it's because we were married the longest, she felt more comfortable with me. Maybe it's because I didn't go crazy when we got divorced, I just . . . I guess I let it happen, gave her whatever she wanted. I guess I . . . right up until it was final . . . I guess I never really believed she'd go through with it. I mean, I didn't even know there were any severe problems."

"Welcome to the club, brother," Tim said. Marshall nodded. Brian looked down into his lap.

"I mean, I worked a lot. My practice was going nuts. She didn't really want anything to do with that, so I was gone a lot."

"I know what you mean," said Costa.

Owen looked at Marshall. "You know, I actually got really pissed at her when she told me you guys had split," he said.

"What are you talking about?" asked Marsh.

"Well, it was typical Violet," Owen said. "And I guess I was just tired of it. The 'it's me not you' thing. And how she thought you were unhappy. I told her to call a spade a spade and be honest with herself. Then last week, she calls me when I'm with you guys—you know how she is."

"Pushy," said Brian.

"Manipulative," said Tim.

"Exactly," Owen blushed. "And to be honest, I . . . well, I . . ."

"You were hoping," Tim said. "Weren't you?"

Owen nodded. He looked up at the other men miserably. "I'm still in love with her." He seemed to fold in on himself then, hunching over the table. "I know, I know," he mumbled. "You guys think I'm nuts." They were silent for a moment. Tim looked down into his lap guiltily. Hadn't he had that punched-in-the-gut feeling himself after seeing Violet the other night? Brian picked at the table top with a fingernail. He didn't like thinking about how he'd felt when Violet left him, and Owen's admission made him do just that. Marshall focused on something across the room, his wounds the rawest of all. Then Costa said, quietly, "She has something, that's for sure." All the men nodded.

"So, what did she want?" asked Tim.

Owen looked around the table. "She wanted to talk about Jake."

chapter 24

Owen stood before the bathroom mirror dabbing at the cut by his eye. He opened the medicine cabinet and pulled out some gauze and Betadine, washed the wound, and applied some triple antibiotic. He snapped a butterfly bandage over the cut to hold it together, then went to work on his lip. It would be sore tomorrow, but it looked like it had stopped bleeding.

He felt like an ass. He thought about all the years he'd made excuses for Violet's behavior so that he could be okay with his feelings for her. He'd always thought of her as a delicate, lively flower that needed protection from the hurts of her past. He told himself he'd forgiven her for leaving him, and that if he could show her how steady and supportive and caring he was, then someday she'd realize the mistake she'd made and come back to him: The one who'd always been there for her.

But he had to be honest with himself. He hadn't forgiven her, not really. Now all his pent-up anger and resentment were bubbling to the surface, manifesting at the most delicate moments.

Jesus, he thought, *now I sound just like Violet, spouting therapeutic bullshit.* Yes, he was angry. For what she'd done to him, and now for what she'd done to the other men as well. Ordinary guys, good guys who'd had to deal with the emotional, mental, and financial damages she'd imposed. Her shoddy excuses for the way she treated people pissed him off.

He knew what he had to do. He gave his face another once-over, then padded to the bedroom and picked up the phone. He sat on the bed and dialed Violet's number.

She answered on the second ring. "Hello?" Her voice sounded muzzy, and Owen imagined her, sleepy-eyed and mussy haired, buried in her blankets.

"Violet, it's Owen."

"Owen?" she sounded alarmed. "What's wrong? Why are you calling so late?"

He took a deep breath, prodding himself on. He was going to do it, and he was going to do it now. "I'm done, Violet."

"Done?"

"With this . . . friend thing . . . or whatever it is."

"Owen! What are you talking about?" She sounded angry, but underneath a little anxious too.

"I mean it. I'm tired of your crap, Violet. And I need to move on. Finally. So, just . . . don't call me anymore. We don't have anything to talk about."

"You're just jealous about Jake . . . still. I told you, you still have feelings for me. You—"

"Violet," Owen said, raising his voice. "I'm serious. I should have said it months—hell, years ago. I'm tired of it, listening to your drama queen rants and pretending like it matters to me. Sick of you taking advantage of my feelings. It's always all about you, Violet. You're selfish, you're a taker, and you've messed up too many lives."

"What the hell are you talking about?" Her voice took on a menacing tone. "Who've you been talking to?"

"I'm talking about me, for a change. Don't call me anymore. And don't show up at my house again. We're through."

On the other end, he could hear Violet sniffling. He shook his head. "And don't try that wounded weepy thing. I'm not falling for it this time," he said, but he knew he had to hang up before it started getting to him. "I have to go," he said.

"Fine," she whispered.

"Good." Owen hung up. He sat on the edge of the bed taking deep breaths. He glanced at the phone, fully expecting her to call back immediately. That was her way, wanting the last word, wanting control of the situation. Maybe he wanted her to call back. But the phone stayed quiet, so he didn't have to wrestle with the question of whether to answer it or not.

He thought about Costa. On the outside he was a big, blustery Greek. But there was substance to him. He'd talked to them about how wrecked he'd been by Violet without any shame. He was remarried, had beautiful kids. He made a choice to move on. Owen laid on his back, his hands behind his head, staring at the ceiling. His body was tense with the possibility of the ringing phone, of Violet's pleading or accusatory voice on the other end of the line. What he had to do was make a choice, like Costa. He had to take charge.

Owen sat up and swung his legs over the side of the bed. He picked up his phone and turned it off, then reached over and unplugged the house phone. If there was an emergency, he decided, the clinic was right there in the front yard, and his clients knew how to reach him. He lay back down, amazed at how his stomach had settled with that one act. He closed his eyes, took a deep breath, and listened to the blessed silence.

chapter 25

Tim couldn't sleep. He felt like a bit of an asshole about how the night had gone. But, damn, what was he supposed to have done? The fact that Owen was still talking to Violet felt like . . . a betrayal somehow. He was supposed to be one of "them," their group, and he was still in the garden with the snake. Then Tim thought about how he'd felt, seeing Violet standing under the streetlight next to Owen. Just the sight of her made him feel like someone had let the air out of him. He was even more upset with himself that seeing her had affected him so much. He knew it had taken a lot of guts for Owen to admit how he felt about Violet. Weren't all of them, maybe, still a little in love with her—with the idea of her, anyway? He saw how crushed Owen had looked when he told them about Violet wanting to find Jake. The other guys surely still had some residual feelings for Violet—especially Marshall, the divorce still fresh.

Jake Bowman. Violet had told Tim more than once during their short time together that in his quiet manner, his geeky-ness, he reminded her a little of her high school sweetheart. Violet enjoyed trying to draw Tim out, as she had with Jake so many years ago, getting him to talk about himself, about how he felt about her. About his family, his work, his dreams.

Tim had been head over heels. Everything about Violet fascinated him. At first, being likened to her "high school sweetheart" was a turn-on, like he was the answer to one of her fantasies. He used to watch her when she slept, her dark hair splayed out on the pillow, her long lashes lying on her cheek, her pink lips. He'd listen to her soft, even breathing and marvel at the fact that a woman as beautiful as Violet was with a big mutt like him.

She was lively, friendly, quick to talk to strangers. And she talked to him, confided in him. It made him feel . . . included in something. She told him about growing up, her sadness, her loneliness, wanting to be closer to her father who was always gone, working. Her mother, The Cold Shoulder, Violet used to call her. She'd had a hard time learning to socialize, she said. Violet used words like that—*socialize, connect, interact.*

She talked about therapy, group work, her first husband Winston and how he was a substitute father figure for her (it took her years to admit that to herself, and tons of therapy, she said). And she talked about Jake. Always Jake. The one that should have been, according to Violet. A bittersweet, adolescent love story. Tim always nodded supportively, but in his head he thought, *Get over it already, it's the past.* It didn't take him long to grow tired of the Jake stories and being compared to the guy who must have been all of seventeen years old at the time. *In fact, when you thought about it like that,* Tim told himself, *it was a goddamned insult.*

Tim used to get up early on Sunday mornings and make Violet blueberry pancakes and coffee with whipped cream floating on top. She'd pad out of the bedroom in her bare feet, wearing only one of his big T-shirts and a pair of her cute panties, and perch on one of the tall chairs at the kitchen counter, her eyes sleepy. He'd kiss her on her maple syrup mouth, and sometimes they would rush back to the bedroom before breakfast was even finished. Back then, Sunday was his favorite day of the week.

Then things got crazy at work. He brought work home, started staying later. He'd come home and Violet would be curled up, already asleep, her abandoned book or the television remote lying on the pillow beside her, and Tim would feel a smidgen of guilt. But, he was moving up in the corporate world, would soon be able to give them a better life. At home, things seemed to be the same to him, Violet seemed the same, albeit more quiet than usual. And then she left.

Violet's abandonment had been sudden, like ripping off a fresh scab. There was no warning. She was simply gone. Tim still had no idea where she'd gone. He'd called her parents and gotten a sarcastic response from her mother. "What did you expect, Tim?" she'd said.

What had he expected? He knew her history. Well, he knew her history as told by Violet. Her former marriages to Costa, Owen, Brian—he'd learned of each man's dark side. Knowing them now gave them a roundness, a realness. A humanness. She'd idolized Winston and had still gotten sad when she talked about him, their time together, the whirling, romantic way they'd met and married. When she talked about his death, she'd still gotten tearful.

She'd also idolized Jake. Violet and Jake met in high school. She said he was sweet and funny and smart. She first noticed him in art class, where he sat next to her at a big table drawing technical sketches of airplanes, boats, and rockets. They were very good. Violet was impressed. She'd watch his hands moving over the paper, his head bent to his task, and imagine what was going on in his mysterious, teenaged boy head.

One day, as they were working on collages, Jake's hand snaked under the table and rested on Violet's thigh. She'd sucked in her breath, suddenly feeling things she'd never felt before. He'd touched her hand, trailing his fingers over hers. Violet looked at him, but his head was still bent over his work, not looking at her. She was confused.

After class she followed him out into the hall, but he'd walked away from her. She stood against her locker, trembling. As the weeks progressed, the gentle, clandestine touching continued. Jake was all Violet could think about. Why wouldn't he talk to her? She asked a friend of his. Jake had a tough time with girls, the friend told her. His mom and dad had gone through a shitty divorce that broke up the family. He lived with his dad in an apartment in town; his mom moved two hundred miles away and took his three sisters with her. He didn't want to get involved with anyone.

Violet took it as a challenge. She would be the one to break through Jake's wall. She would show him what it was like to be loved. Jake would blush crimson at her attention. Violet would melt with the cuteness of it. She wrote him letters, sent him cards. This went on all through high school, and while the two developed a friendship, hung with the same crowd, went places together, they'd never dated.

After high school, Jake joined the service and left. Violet was heartbroken. She moped for a while, then started dating other boys. About eight months after leaving, Violet received a letter from Jake. It was the beginning of a four-year correspondence between them, and even though Jake continued writing, he wouldn't admit more than a friendly fondness for Violet. When

Winston came along, sweeping Violet off her feet, she allowed herself to be swept.

Tim sat staring at the computer screen. So, now Violet was planning on seeing Jake. He wondered where the guy was, and if he knew Violet's intentions. And he wondered, as he had more than once before, what it was that this guy had that so intrigued Violet. What did Jake have that none of them had?

Early the next morning, Tim picked up his cell and scrolled down his contact list until he found Marshall.

"Hey, man," Marshall answered sleepily. "What time is it?"

Tim looked at the clock on the computer screen. "Sorry, Marsh. It's seven."

"What's up?"

"Hey, first off, sorry about last night," Tim said. "I was an asshole. I shoulda just asked Owen about it that night. Or called you, or something."

"I'm glad you didn't call me," Marshall said. "I probably would have gone to his house and pounded him and ended up in jail or something."

"Yeah," Tim said. "Still. I could have handled it better."

"I agree there, bro," Marshall said, chuckling. "So, what's up?"

"I was thinking . . ." Tim hesitated.

"Yeah?" asked Marshall. "What about?"

"Jake."

"What about him?"

Tim chewed on his lip, suddenly regretting the phone call. This guy was going to think he was nuts. He took a breath. "Owen said Violet's thinking about looking him up."

"So?"

"So, maybe we should first," Tim said carefully. "You know, you and me and the guys?"

"What the hell for?"

"Well, I . . . don't know . . . exactly," Tim said.

Marshall sounded suddenly interested. "Well, what are you thinking?"

"I was thinking about the stuff Violet told all of us about each other. Not the best stuff always, right?"

"Right."

"Well, think about it. We're all—pretty okay, right?" Tim said. "I mean, we had that thing last night, but we've kind of been . . . getting along, you know? Like . . . friends."

"Yeah," Marsh said, but still not following Tim's line of thought.

"Violet always thought of Jake as 'the one that got away,' right? She told Owen she's tired of making mistakes—like we were all mistakes. But maybe *she* was the mistake. For all of us. I mean, I was wrecked by her. And listen man, I admire you for keeping it together the way you are, but I know you're messed up, too, or you never would have tried to cream Owen last night. And look at Brian. The guy was seriously fucked up."

"Okay," Marshall said carefully, thinking about the hubcap-covered ranch-style in the boondocks.

"I guess what I'm saying, in the name of, I don't know, brotherhood, I guess—shouldn't we maybe, warn this guy or something?"

There was silence on the other end of the phone. Then, "I don't know, man."

They both hung on the phone, not talking. Tim clicked around on his computer screen. Marshall broke the silence.

"Where's he at?"

"I don't know," said Tim, clicking the mouse, his eyes hot on the computer screen, "but I can find out."

chapter 26

Brian's mother had been calling the restaurant constantly to ask him when he was quitting the foolishness and coming home. He knew he should drive up to see her, but he just didn't feel ready. Every time he imagined her squinting face, the cigarette paused on her lip, the varied muumuus she liked to wear, he broke out in a cold sweat. He was just getting his pins under him, had started a new friendship, and maybe more, with Jenny. And anyway, his house had been listed—at least his mom had done that for him, although she told him the realtor hadn't been happy that he wouldn't be coming back to put the house into what she called "livable condition."

Brian was in the kitchen with Niki preparing the specials, pastitsio and roasted chickens with lemons and garlic. It was the first time Niki had let Brian prepare them on his own, and he was more than a little nervous. He wanted to get it right and make his mentor proud. Costa purposely stayed out of the kitchen, going into the office to work on some of the accounts and ordering he'd gotten behind on. The kid was nervous enough without the big Greek staring over his shoulder.

Bettina, the daytime hostess, came back to the kitchen to tell Brian his mom was calling again. She flipped her glossy red ponytail over her shoulder. Brian could tell by the set of her mouth that she was pissed. "I told her you were busy, like you said, but man, she's pushy. I'm not dealing with her anymore." She turned to leave the kitchen and called over her shoulder. "You're going to have to call her back, Brian. This is bullshit. I have stuff to do."

Brian looked up from a pot of boiling pasta. He was worried about overcooking it. "Tell her I'll call her back."

Bettina turned to him impatiently. "You know, I did that last time. This is like the third time she's called this morning. She's just going to—"

"I can't talk now," Brian said, stiffly.

"Jesus Christ," Bettina said, huffing back out the kitchen door. "She's really starting to piss me off."

"Join the club," Brian said under his breath as Bettina walked away.

That afternoon, a woman breezed into the kitchen with Bettina right on her heels. "You can't go in there!" Bettina said.

"Hey, what's going on?" Costa asked, stepping from the stove toward the kitchen door.

"Are you Brian Jankowicz?" the woman said. She was looking at Costa over her black-framed glasses, her stylishly cut hair swinging in her face. She was wearing an expensively cut suit and heels and looked entirely out of place in the kitchen.

"Sonny boy," Costa said, not taking his eyes off the woman. She reminded him of a bug he'd seen once, a praying mantis. "Come here."

Brian didn't like the look of her either. She was older, but her face was tight, and she was wearing a ton of makeup. She looked like a cartoon character to him, from one of those new, badly drawn cartoons, not the cool Looney Tunes he used to watch as a kid. She put her hand on her hip as he came toward her. "Mr. Jankowicz?" she asked. Her manner said step it up, I'm in a goddamned hurry.

Brian stared at her. No one had called him Mr. Jankowicz before, except the high school principal that one time when he got in trouble for putting cherry bombs in the girls' bathroom. Walking toward this woman now felt exactly the same as walking to the principal's office that day.

"Yeah?" he said, swallowing hard. "I'm Brian." He wiped his sweaty hands on the front of his apron.

The woman stuck out her hand and grasped his hard, pumping it. "Maureen Bannister-Briggs," she said. "I represent George D. Applewhite the third."

"Um . . . okay," Brian said nervously, wiping his hands on the front of his apron again. The only time he'd heard a line like that was in court. This had to be trouble. Ms. Bannister-Briggs arched her eyebrows at him in a way that made him feel like he had to go to the bathroom.

"Is there somewhere we can talk privately?" she asked, adjusting her large glasses on her nose.

Brian looked at Costa helplessly. "You can use my office," Costa said, looking at the woman suspiciously. "What's this about, huh?"

"Sir," said Maureen Bannister-Briggs. "This is a private matter for Mr. Jankowicz."

"No." Said Brian quickly. "It's okay to talk in front of Costa." He looked at Costa, pleading. "Okay?" Costa shrugged and wiped his hands on a towel.

"As you wish," said Ms. Bannister-Briggs.

"This way," Costa said, showing her the way to the office.

Once seated in the office on Costa's large leather sofa, Ms. Bannister-Briggs took a file out of her briefcase. "Mr. Jankowicz," she said. "I'd asked your mother to contact you several times in the past couple of weeks, but it appears she has not done so."

Brian thought about the three phone calls he'd begged off of just that morning. "What's this about?" he asked.

"Your house," she said simply.

"The silverdome?" Costa asked, incredulously.

"Um . . . yes." Ms. Bannister-Briggs looked at Costa as if he were a fly on her salad.

"Do you know who George Applewhite is, Mr. Jankowicz?" she said this as if she felt sorry for Brian.

Brian shook his head.

"As I suspected," said Bannister-Briggs. She took a pamphlet out of the file and handed it to Brian. On the cover was a photograph of a stuffy-looking man with thinning hair and a bad necktie. Under the photograph was the caption:

THE GEORGE D. APPLEWHITE FOUNDATION FOR
ARTISTIC ADVANCEMENT.

Brian looked at her, confused. "I don't understand."

"Mr. Applewhite is very interested in your work."

"My . . . what?"

"Your work. The . . . um . . . metal collages." She said, and when Brian still looked at her blankly, she went on. "In and on your house. In . . . what's the name of that village?"

"Omer," Brian and Costa said together.

"My *work*?" Brian said again.

"Yes," said Ms. Bannister-Briggs, as if Brian was a very slow child. "And if I must say so myself, although I am not much of a collage aficionado, brilliant."

Costa put his hand over his mouth to keep from laughing aloud. Brian looked at him, open-mouthed.

"Brilliant?" Brian said, still not understanding.

"Very much so, I must say. So, Mr. Jankowicz, the reason I am here is to make you an offer." She sat back on the leather sofa for dramatic pause. "Mr. Applewhite is prepared to offer you one hundred thousand for the house, and he is interested in commissioning you for a large collage slash metal sculpture for the new building he just purchased in Detroit. Your metal sculptures are definitely on track toward the trend of recycled art—green art, if you will."

Brian started laughing. "Okay," he said. "You got me. Who put you up to this? The guys?" He looked at Costa. "You in on this, too?"

Costa raised his hands helplessly. "No, sonny boy. Not me."

"Mr. Jankowicz!" Ms. Bannister-Briggs said. "I assure you this is no joke." She opened the file again and took out a document and pushed it toward Brian. "This should explain everything. You should have your attorney peruse it before signing. Of course, this does not include the commission work. We simply want to get started on the property. Mr. Applewhite intends to turn it into an artist's retreat. Brian held the contract in his hands, which had begun to tremble. There were dollar amounts on the pages. Big dollar amounts. He pointed to them, holding the documents up for Costa to see. The big man was up, patting him on the back exuberantly. "Sonny boy!" he said. "You're a fucking genius!"

chapter 27

The first weekend in November dawned crisp and clear. Marshall pulled up just as Owen, with Bentley in tow, bounded out of Owen's Navigator. Bentley went right over to Marshall and gave him a sloppy head butt, then sat looking up at him, wagging his tail expectantly. Marshall broke out into a grin and promptly squatted down and gave the mutt a vigorous scratch behind his floppy ears. "How you doin', buddy?" he said to the dog. He looked up at Owen. "This our new teammate?" Bentley gave Marshall a sloppy dog kiss on the cheek.

Owen laughed. "Looks like he picked you for his team, for sure."

Marshall popped up and shook Owen's hand. "How are you doin', man?"

"Not bad."

Marshall dropped his eyes. "Look," he said. "About the other night—"

Owen shrugged. "Don't worry about it," he said. "I can see where you were coming from." The two stood awkwardly, avoiding eye contact for a few moments, before they spotted the other guys in the park.

They walked into the park. Costa, Brian, and Tim were already there, sitting at a picnic table with a huge cooler filled with beers and lunch prepared by Costa. Marshall shook his head and smiled. *That guy sure knows how to take care of people*, he thought. An afternoon of football had been Brian's idea. The guys had been quick to accept. It was good to see the nervous young man opening up and initiating something. That took confidence and faith in their friendships. Even if it wasn't something they talked about, the fact that they were making efforts to see each other regularly made it clear.

As Marshall, Owen, and Bentley approached, the youngest man's eyes lit up. He stepped back from the picnic table and held out his hands to receive the ball.

"You sure?" Owen called, glancing down at Bentley. He knew where this would lead.

Brian clapped his hands together then held them up again. "Right here, bro!" Owen laughed.

"Okay," he called. "Your funeral!" He threw the ball and Bentley barked, bounding after it. Brian caught the ball squarely in his chest, his arms clasped protectively around it, and turned on one leg, graceful as a ballerina, as the canine, tongue hanging out happily, crashed into him, sending Brian and the ball sprawling.

"Tackle!" Marshall and Tim threw their arms up in the air. Costa laughed, clutching his belly. Owen grinned and turned, catching Tim's eye. Tim's smile faded somewhat, and the two men stared at one another. In the meantime, Bentley sprinted calmly around Brian's prostrate form, grabbed the ball between his paws, and lay down on it. He looked expectantly at Owen, his tail thumping. Brian rolled over and patted the dog on the head. "Good one, boy!" he said.

Marshall turned, seeing Owen and Tim's locked gaze. He patted Owen on the shoulder. "Looks like our team has the ball," he said, inclining his head toward the vet's dog.

Owen cleared his throat, his focus falling away from Tim, and gave Marshall a crooked smile. He clapped his hands. "Come on, you old bag of bones!" he said, and Bentley came bounding toward him, leaving the football behind. Brian swooped it up, the smile on his face melting the years away, making him look like a ten-year-old kid. He headed toward the vacant soccer field. "Let's hit it!" he hollered back at the other men.

Costa waved a hand over the picnic table. "I'm gonna stay here and—"

"Oh, no, you don't!" Marshall have him a playful shove toward the field, where Owen and Brian were already passing the ball back and forth, Bentley leaping happily between them. "Let's go, old man."

"If I break my old Greek ass—"

"Go on, you baby." Marshall laughed at him, following. He stopped and looked back at Tim. He was finishing a can of soda. "You coming?"

"Sure," Tim said, setting the empty on the table and trudging toward Marshall.

"What gives, man?"

Tim shook his head. "I'm cool," he said.

"Hey," Marshall said, "Owen's okay."

"I know." Tim sighed. He jogged toward the field. Owen had the ball and was about to pass it to Brian's waiting hands. Tim whistled loudly and waved. "Right here, Owen!"

Owen paused for a split second, then turned to Tim and threw the ball. Tim caught it neatly. "Head's up!" He threw it to Costa, who was turned watching some pretty girls passing the field. The ball hit him in the shoulder, and all the guys laughed at him. "Hey, pops! Eyes on the ball!" Marshall shouted at him, and the women giggled at Costa and waved.

They broke off into informal teams—Marshall, Owen, and Bentley against Tim, Costa, and Brian, though Bentley indiscriminately played for both sides, depending on who had his beloved football. The guys threw, passed, blocked, and tackled, using the abandoned soccer posts as goals until they were all grass-stained and thirsty. Costa was leaning on one of the goal posts catching his breath while Brian and Marshall headed toward the picnic table for something to drink. Tim sat with his back up against the opposite post. Owen was stretched out in the grass near him, his eyes closed against the sun, catching his breath. "I'm getting old," he wheezed.

"You?" Costa said, "You got nothin' on this old *papou*."

Owen turned his head and shaded his eyes with a hand. "Did you say you are a poo-poo?"

Costa waved a hand dismissively. "*Papou!*" he said. "An old grandpa! I'm not ready for that yet. I'm getting a beer."

Owen chuckled at him, and he and Tim watched the older man walk away. For a moment the silence was thick between them, the others making small talk, laughing and popping the tops of beer cans back at the picnic area. Owen sat up and swung around. "Look—" he said.

"No, man," Tim interrupted. "Hey, I—"

Owen put his hands up. "No, I get it. I get it. I would have been ticked off at me, too. About the Violet thing."

"Look, whatever you do is your business and I—"

"No, no," Owen insisted. "I was . . ." he looked away and let out a huge sigh, "delusional, I guess."

Tim leaned forward. "I get it, man."

"I don't think you do," said Owen. "I mean, you've been . . . away from her. I stayed connected." He looked toward the picnic area. Bentley was begging Marshall shamelessly for potato chips. "But that's changed now," he said.

Tim's eyebrows scrunched together. "What do you mean?"

Owen looked at the other man. "I told her we're through. With the . . . friendship. Whatever it is. I can't do it anymore."

"Wow." Tim leaned back, nodding and watching Owen.

"Yeah," said Owen, picking at his thumbnail.

Tim reached over and patted his shoulder. "Good for you," he said.

"Thanks." Owen stuck a hand out. "Sorry we got off to a bad start."

Tim grasped the other man's hand firmly. "Me, too." Then he jumped as the football landed squarely between them. "What the—"

Brian bounded toward them laughing. "What're you ladies talking about?"

"I'll show you ladies!" Tim jumped up and tackled Brian as the others made their way back to the field, and it was game on once again, Bentley happily barking and running amok between them. It didn't take long for them to collapse, out of breath, after a few more minutes of play. Owen, Brian, and Marshall were stretched out in the grass under an impossibly beautiful autumn sun. Bentley had his head tucked in Owen's armpit. The dog had immediately fallen asleep and was now snoring loudly. Costa stood with his hands on his hips, surveying the park, and Tim was sitting cross-legged in the grass.

Marshall squinted against the sun, looking at the other guys. He hadn't felt this relaxed in a long time. And even though he was with these men who'd been married to Violet, he hadn't thought about her once while they threw the ball around. He took in a deep breath. Today, even Tim and Owen, who'd been cagey around one another from the get-go, seemed more at ease with each other.

These are good guys, Marshall thought to himself. He thought about the fact that while Violet had picked men who were all quite different from one another in many ways, the common denominator was they were all good people. Marshall thought about Tim's idea. If they were good guys, Jake undoubtedly was, too. And now Violet was planning on sweeping through his life, surely causing her particular brand of chaos. The guy might have resisted her in high school, but now she'd had six men to practice her wiles on. He didn't have a chance.

Costa looked at the other men. "Hungry?" They all turned to him and chuckled. "What? What?" he said, holding up his palms. "It's what I do, okay?"

"Okay, okay," said Marshall, getting up and brushing grass off his jeans. The others followed suit and headed toward the picnic table.

They were all on a second beverage when Marshall said, "Hey, Tim, tell the guys your idea about Jake."

✳ ✳ ✳

Owen wasn't sure about this. Hunting up Jake before Violet could? He wasn't sure that would benefit any of them—or Jake for that matter. He shoved his backpack into the trunk of the Navigator, looking back at the other guys packing up their stuff. Bentley had his nose on the front window and was looking out pitifully at his new friends. Owen knew he'd be fine as soon as he got him home to his bowls of food and water. But it wasn't the dog that was niggling at him—it was the whole prospect of the trip. Owen liked the guys, sure, for the most part—Tim still kind of bugged him. Owen wasn't sure why, exactly. It was more than the stolen parking spot, or even that he'd outed him to the other guys about Violet. Maybe it was the fact that he was the one she'd gone to after him.

Despite his vacillating feelings about Tim, he was glad he'd told him about the conversation with Violet. He'd thought about that night a lot in the past few days, the finality with which he'd hung up on her, his words. His head and his heart wrestled, causing a tangled ball of confusion in his gut, and that confusion made him edgy and short-tempered. Just this week he'd snapped at his assistant, Tanya, twice. The first time she'd let it go, but the second time the big woman had stepped up to him, her eyes flashing, and he knew he'd better back off. He'd seen that woman hold down a two-hundred-pound mastiff.

Sure, Jake was probably a good guy. However, despite a brotherly intention of "saving" him from Violet, Owen saw him as just one more rival for her affections. Owen was the one who'd invested the most in Violet, and he was pissed that now some other guy held her attention. So, he'd said some harsh things—had, in fact, broken off the friendship. But since when did Violet listen to him, or anyone for that matter? It was all about what she wanted. Still, he thought worriedly, she hadn't tried to contact him since that night. Maybe he'd pushed too far. He slunk behind the steering wheel and pulled out of the parking lot. Maybe that had been what she wanted—to have Owen out of her life. And maybe he'd played right into her hands.

Now, he'd agreed to be a part of this Jake thing. If Violet knew about this, it would really piss her off. He glanced in his rearview mirror to see the other guys getting in their vehicles. Why hadn't he voiced his opinion instead of agreeing to driving them, for christsake? He knew full well the why of it—he wanted the guys to like him. It was like elementary school all over again, the boys against the girls. He shook his head, then reached over and gave Bentley a comforting pat. "Your person is an idiot," he told the dog. "A big, fat idiot."

PROGRESS NOTES: Violet VanDahmm

    CASE NUMBER: V2011-100982

    DATE: 11-07-2011

SUMMARY:

Violet was in a state of high excitement. She immediately spoke about Jake and said that he had finally responded to her and that she'd gotten a home address from him on the pretext of adding him to her holiday card list. She stated now that she had the address, she would go forward with her plans to drive there (Petoskey) to "surprise" him. I asked her to talk about her communication with Jake, and she stated that he had responded to an email saying that if she were "ever in the area," it might be "nice to see her sometime." Violet described her mood as "over the moon" and "happier that I've been in a long time" because Jake "has obviously missed me, too!"

I stated that while his response was cordial, I found it somewhat cool. I additionally expressed concern that she'd gotten his address by telling Jake a "white lie." Violet ignored the concern and stated that I "just don't know Jake" and that she could "read his underlying message." I urged her to take some more time and have some clearer communication with Jake prior to planning a trip to see him, but Violet insisted that she was "determined to begin" her "new life."

I attempted to refocus her on her recurring issue with Owen, which she passed off, saying that she was "over that" and that they were no longer friends. She went into a reverie about past history with Jake, from which she could not be swayed.

When asked about her journaling work, Violet became somewhat embarrassed. She stated that she does not want to journal, and that the book is still blank. She said she will return it and that I should give the book to someone else who can use it—that she only benefits from "talk therapy." I asked her to tell me in what positive ways her life has changed since beginning therapy with this office. I stated that it was my feeling that she has not made any changes, nor done any introspection or work as suggested, and that she is simply using me as a sounding board. Violet became teary then and stated, "You don't like me!"

We talked about some basic goals for future therapy, if she chooses to continue.

Yolanda H. Malik, LCSW
Champoor and Associates

chapter 28

The five men coordinated their schedules, deciding to leave early on Saturday. Tim and Costa, who hadn't wanted to look foolish to their families, concocted a story about the five of them going deer hunting. They'd be traveling on opening weekend and would blend in with the thousands of other male travelers heading to the great outdoors to bag their buck or doe.

It would be a lot of driving, nearly six hundred miles round-trip, but they'd agreed to switch up, each taking a leg of the journey. It'd been an especially hard sell for Costa, convincing Angelina that he would leave Niki alone on their busiest night of the week and forego church and a family dinner on Sunday for "hunting" with the guys. "Hunting?" she'd said. "Since when do you hunt?"

"Hey," he'd said. "Michigan. Water wonderland. Hunting. Fishing. I'm gettin' old. I shouldn't have some fun?" He'd kissed her on the neck, which always melted her, and promised her he'd make time to do something special with her and the kids when he got back.

"Go," she said. "I don't know who these guys are, but hanging with them is sure good for you."

"Good? Good how?"

"You're smiling more. She snuggled in close and put her arms around him. And you're more—I don't know, baby. You're more relaxed. Or happy. Or something. You're more here for me," she said, looking into Costa's eyes. "Do you know what I mean?"

"I think so," he said. He held her tight. "Angie, you're the best thing that ever happened to me, you know that, right?"

"You're right," she said, smiling. "I am. Now, get outta here." She slapped him on the butt and winked.

✳ ✳ ✳

Tim had invited the group for a homemade breakfast before they hit the road early on Saturday morning. Jenny'd volunteered to care for their parents for the weekend. She'd been different lately, a little softer around the edges. Quietly happy. This morning she showed up with bags full of groceries, dressed in a low-cut sweater and jeans tighter than Tim ever remembered seeing on her. "What's up, sis?" he said, grinning. He knew damn well what was up. He smiled as he thought about seeing his sister and new buddy just last week, sitting on the porch swing together after their date, even though it was frosty outside, holding hands, talking quietly.

"Nothing's up," she said, punching him in the arm. "Just thought I'd come over, you know, help out. Make you guys breakfast."

Tim arched his eyebrow. "Really?" He gestured at her new sweater. It was red and had a big, soft collar that showed off her neck and shoulders. She slapped at him.

"Yes, really. Can't a sister support her brother?"

"More like my sister wants to support her brother's friend. Not mentioning any names." He chuckled.

Jenny got busy making the guys a feast of French toast, sausage, bacon, and scrambled eggs with onions and green peppers. She'd dug mom's old coffee urn out of the basement and the twenty-cupper was busily perking away.

Costa and Brian arrived first, Brian coming shyly into the back door and nodding at Jenny, who beamed when she saw him. Costa nudged Brian. "Nice," he said softly.

"Cut it out," Brian said, lowering his eyes to the carpet.

Costa introduced himself to Jenny, making a big deal of kissing her hand and making her blush. "You need help, sweetheart?" he said. "You know, Brian here is training in my kitchen."

Jenny looked over at Brian, smiling. "I could use some help," she said. Brian shrugged off his plaid jacket and joined her at the counter. Their heads were soon together as they talked softly, Jenny stirring up the giant pan of scrambled eggs and Brian plating up mounds of French toast and bacon. Tim poured Costa a cup of coffee, and they took a place at the table. Costa loaded his with cream and sugar.

"Good," Costa said to Jenny, holding the cup aloft.

"Thanks. But how can you tell with all that crap in it?"

Costa laughed. "She's got spunk," he said to Tim. "I like that. Just like my Angie." He gave Brian a wink, and the younger man turned pink and focused on the heaping platter of bacon.

There was a knock on the kitchen door. Marshall and Owen came in, and Jenny offered them some coffee. They pulled up chairs at the big kitchen table.

Jenny and Brian started bringing food to the table. Tim's father appeared in the doorway. He shuffled along on a four-pronged cane, his wavy hair wild around his head, making him resemble Albert Einstein. He scratched at his fish-white belly, which protruded slightly from the bottom of his white T-shirt and the blue cardigan sweater that was buttoned across its expanse. "Hey," he said. "Just like Christmas." He looked around at the new faces. "Except for I seem to have a few extra kids."

"Sit down, Daddy," Jenny said, pulling out a seat at the head of the table for her father. "This is our dad, Jerry, everyone."

"Get your mom," Jerry said. "She would get a kick out of this. Plus look at this breakfast! You make all this, baby girl?"

"No, kiddin'," Costa chimed in. "You need a job, beautiful?"

"Yes, daddy." Jenny smiled with pride at the compliments. Brian reached over and squeezed her shoulder, making her beam even more.

Tim looked at Jenny, questioning, then back to his father. "Oh, Dad," Tim said. "I don't know. You know Mom hasn't had a meal out here since—"

"Go on. Listen to your father," Costa broke in. "Get your mamma."

"Yeah," Jerry said. "She'd enjoy this."

Tim and Jenny looked at each other over the heads of their guests. Jenny shrugged her shoulders at her older brother. "I'll go help her get dressed," she said. "Then you can help her out here, Tim."

"Excellent," said Costa, beaming. "Family."

A few moments later, Tim wheeled his mother out into the kitchen and got her settled by his dad. Jenny had helped her put on her best robe and brushed her hair back from her face in soft waves. She had a blanket over her knees and was smiling and nodding at the group gathered around the kitchen table. "Everybody, this is my mom, Elise." He introduced the guys. Elise was aflutter with the attention from everyone. They were all talking at once and eating, and Tim thought that it did feel a little like Christmas morning. It was a good feeling.

"So," Elise said, "how do all you boys know each other?"

The table went suddenly silent. Tim, Owen, Marshall, Costa, and Brian all looked at each other. "Well . . ." Tim began.

Jenny broke in. "What you have here, Mom," she said, "is the Recovery from Violet support group." She grinned mischievously.

"Jen!" Tim warned.

"Violet?" Elise said. "Violet Benjamin?"

Marshall cleared his throat. "Violet Benjamin Montgomery Pavlos Jankowicz Blanton Stark VanDahmm, to be exact. Ma'am."

Elise pointed her fork all around the table. "All of you were married to Violet?" she asked, which was met with solemn nods. Elise looked at her husband. "Remember what she did to our Tim?"

"She was pretty, though," Jerry said.

"Jerry!"

"Sorry, Mamma," Jerry said. He elbowed Costa, who was sitting next to him. "She was though, huh?"

Costa nodded. "Beautiful," he agreed.

"Hmph," Elise fumed. "Nothing beautiful about what she did to our boy!"

"Mom—" Tim started.

"You were a wreck. I had a feeling about her. I told you, Timmy."

"Mom. Please." He looked around the table, embarrassed. He could see the other guys were embarrassed for him, and somehow that made it all the worse.

"More French toast, anybody?" Jen said brightly, holding up the platter. Tim shot her a grateful look.

"Okay," said Elise. "I get it. I'll shut up. But, what are you boys doing about any of it?"

They all looked at each other. "Um . . . going . . . hunting," Owen said weakly.

"You're going to kill her?" shouted Elise.

There was a moment of silence, then they all started laughing.

"No, Mom!" Tim said. "We're just, you know, hanging out." He let out a weak chuckle. "You know, supporting each other."

"Supporting?" his mom said. "Like a . . . therapy group?" Elise crinkled up her nose.

"Kinda."

"I saw that on Oprah," she said, nodding knowingly. She narrowed her eyes at the men. "Mostly women do that kind of thing, though."

"Yeah," said Owen. He sighed.

"So, what are you boys hunting?" Jerry asked. "Deer season, isn't it?"

Tim looked at his dad. "Yep! We're going to try and get us a buck."

"Hey, take my old Winchester," his dad said. "Probably needs a cleaning, but she's still a nice piece. Got a couple a boxes of ammo for her, too."

"Sure," Tim gulped. "Thanks, Dad."

The men all turned to look at Tim. The last thing they needed to be taking on this trip was a gun, but no one said a word.

chapter 29

They piled into Owen's Lincoln Navigator, the good food and the family camaraderie they'd shared at the table getting them off to a great start. Costa sat up front with Marshall, while Brian, Tim, and Owen squeezed in the back seat. Brian sat next to the window, watching the fields slide by. They were listening to an oldies station, and Bachman-Turner Overdrive was taking care of business.

Brian leaned his head against the window, staring as they passed cow pastures, junkyards, road signs, and newly barren fields of corn. He'd asked Costa to keep quiet about his windfall. Brian wasn't sure why he didn't want to tell the other guys, exactly. He figured he would, eventually, but for now the news was his.

The signed contract was stuck into the frame of the mirror over the dresser in the room he rented from Costa and Angelina. At night, he kept taking it down from its spot, and he would lie in bed staring at it with the light from the bedside lamp shining through it. He could start a new life—with money he made with his own hands, from something he created. He wasn't sure exactly how he felt about that yet, but he did know he was filled with a kind of wonder. That out of his pain he'd made something that mattered to someone, instead of something to be ridiculed.

Everyone's bellies were full, the car was warm, and the movement lulling. Costa had his arm slung across the back of the seat and was tapping his fingers in time to the music. The miles slid by. Before long, Marshall's head lolled on the back of the seat, and he was snoring.

It hadn't taken Tim long to find Jake's Landscaping and its blocky, basic website. Just a homepage with a generic photo of greenery and the address for the business. Learning anything more about Jake had proved more challenging. Tim had checked Facebook, MySpace, Twitter, and LinkedIn, but the man had no social networking page—virtually unheard of in this day and age. But he kept searching. He leaned against the car door, typing into search engines on his iPhone, while outside the car, the gorgeous autumn forests and fields slid by.

Up front, Marshall leaned against the headrest, his eyes closed to the bright sunlight. He still wasn't sleeping the best, and the movement of the call lulled him. He thought about how jealous he'd gotten the first time Violet talked to him about Jake Bowman. They'd been seeing each other for about four weeks and had just been out to dinner and had seen the movie *Love Actually*, which featured that English guy he couldn't stand, Hugh Grant. He had gigantic teeth and always played the witty ladies man. Marshall just didn't see it. Violet loved the movie and was wiping her running eyes as they walked hand in hand out of the theatre.

She asked him what his favorite part of the movie was. "The little boy was good," he'd said. He didn't want to tell Violet his favorite parts of the movie were the scenes that contained that British hottie Martine McCutcheon, whom Violet slightly resembled.

Violet sighed. It was Liam Neeson she loved, she'd said. He reminded her so much of Jake. The wistful look in her eyes made Marshall's jealousy flare.

"Who's Jake?" he'd demanded.

"The one that got away," Violet said, with a sad smile. "His eyes are like Liam's," she said. "Sad."

They'd gotten in an argument, their first. Marshall'd thought at first that Jake was some other guy Violet was seeing, and while they hadn't specifically discussed being exclusive, Marshall had thought they were. Couldn't Violet tell how he felt about her?

Violet explained how in love she'd been with Jake in high school, and she told Marshall he had nothing to worry about. She'd even been pretty turned on that he'd gotten so jealous. Marshall remembered an awesome round of lovemaking that night in Violet's tiny loft apartment.

It wouldn't have been a problem, but she brought it up a lot. When they'd really started fighting about it, Violet went through another round of group therapy, Lost Loves Group, or some such nonsense. At least that one had only cost ten bucks a week, instead of the seventy-five an hour that quack from Family Care Services, Inc., charged later in their marriage. Marshall remembered more than once swearing he was just going to take a hundred dollar bill and fling it out the car window every other week, for all the good therapy did Violet or their relationship. Thank God he hadn't let her persuade him to go as well. Twice as much money out the window.

Up front, the Bee Gees were whining about night fever. Costa grimaced and started flipping through radio stations. "What the hell are you doing?" Owen said.

Costa's eyebrows arched. "You fucking kidding?" Costa said.

Owen flushed. "I kinda liked the movie," he said.

"Fucking Saturday Night Fever?" Costa was laughing. "Okay, John Travolta." Costa cranked the radio and began chair dancing in the front seat. Tim reached forward and tapped Marshall awake. Marshall and Tim began singing in falsetto, "The night fever, night fever: We know how to do it. Gimme the night fever, night fever: We know how to show it."

In tandem, Costa, Marshall, and Tim pointed toward the roof of the car. "Pick an apple, pick an apple, pick an apple," Tim chanted, reaching for the ceiling, then down low to the floor in time to the music, mimicking Travolta's famous dance floor move from the film. Brian was laughing so hard he was bent over in his seat."Knock it the fuck off!" said Owen, snapping off the radio. For a second the car was silent, then all the men burst out laughing. "You fuckin' idiots," Owen said.

"We're idiots?" Costa said. "Bet you're the only one of us has a snow white polyester leisure suit hanging in his closet at home."

Owen looked at Costa. "And I look fucking stunning in it," he said, as the carful of men burst out laughing again.

✳ ✳ ✳

Big Bear Brewery was full of deer hunters telling their tales of the morning hunt, how many got away and how many got bagged. They were a noisy, scruffy bunch, and Marshall, Costa, Tim, Brian, and Owen blended right into the crowd in their plaid flannels, jeans, and boots. They were sitting at one of the gigantic pine plank tables working their way through burgers and nursing their beers, which came to them in huge glasses shaped like boots.

A busty waitress came over wearing a T-shirt emblazoned with BRRRRR BEER BOOTS. She cleared what she could from their table. "How'd you boys do this morning?" she asked. "See anything?"

The men looked at each other. "I saw a few does," Brian said finally. "No doe permit though."

"Isn't that just the way?" the waitress said. "Get you boys anything?"

"I think we're good," Tim said.

"Okay," she said brightly. "Just give me a yell when you want those beers refilled."

Costa watched her leave the table. "We are drinking beer from shoes," he said. "Unbelievable."

"I think it's kind of cool," said Brian.

"Well, don't get any ideas, sonny boy," Costa said. "I don't even want plastic glasses in my restaurant, much less these crazy things."

Tim let out a big belch. "That was the best burger I ever had in my friggin' life."

"Ditto," said Owen. "Elk burger with jalapeños. Man."

Marshall had been quiet through most of the meal. Now he spoke. "So, we're finally going to meet Jake." He paused and looked at the others. "What do you think he's like?"

For a moment everyone was quiet, then Tim said, "Us."

"Right," said Owen. "Although for the record, being the one who was married to Violet the longest, I figure I was subjected to the most stories—but, now that I think about it, they were more about her than about him."

"She didn't talk to me about him much," Brian said. "A couple of times. Kind of bothered me though. She sure didn't want me talking about any ex-girlfriends."

"But, if you remember, according to Violet herself, she and Jake weren't even an item," Marshall said. "Just friends. Maybe this guy is a lot smarter than we are."

"No shit there," said Costa.

"What was that book or movie or something that came out a couple of years ago?" Tim asked. "*He's Just Not That Into You?*"

"Yeah," Marshall said. "That was it."

"Well, maybe it was a case of Violet just not being able to get through her head that he wasn't into her."

"And maybe," said Costa, "it was, you know, you want most what you can't have. Think about it."

"Why didn't he just dump her then? As a friend and everything?" Brian asked. "Just rip off the Band-Aid. She sure had no trouble doing that to any of us."

"Exactly," said Owen. "They wrote back and forth for years. Then she just lost track of him. You know Violet. What a flake." Owen fiddled with his napkin. "I used to think that was cute, you know?"

"Yeah," Marshall said. "So did I. She was always losing her keys, too. I don't know how many spares I kept around just in case."

"Yeah," Costa said. "So, what are we going to do?"

"Well, she's intending to go see him," said Owen. "That's what she told me. I guess we're . . . warning the guy?"

"And seeing what he's about," said Tim. "I want to know how this guy resisted her. None of us could."

"Those eyes," Costa said, "like fire."

"Yeah," said Brian. "Yeah."

"Well, shit," said Owen. "Let's get back on the road and just figure it out when we get there. I mean, let's be realistic. We basically want to see what this guy's like, right? Because we're . . ." he stopped.

"Jealous," Marshall finished. "He kept her attention all this time. And we couldn't."

"Right," said Costa.

"And hey," said Owen. "If nothing else, road trip, right?" Owen looked out the window. He felt a little shitty. He cared less about Jake and more about Violet. If he was being honest with himself, he was half hoping he might run into her on the trip.

Marshall smacked him on the shoulder, and Owen jumped. "Uh, dude, you coming with us?" Owen's face reddened at his reverie. The other guys were moving out of their chairs and putting on their coats.

"Um . . . yeah," he said. He stood and threw some bills on the table, adding to the stack the others had left.

They headed toward the door.

"Where are we staying when we get up there anyway?" asked Brian.

Marshall looked at Tim, who looked at Owen, then back at Marshall. "Um . . . I thought you . . ."

"Well, I thought *you* found someplace."

Brian's eyes widened. "Oh, man, we're screwed."

"What do you mean, we're screwed?" said Owen. "It's the friggin' vacation wonderland. We'll just find a motel or something when we get there."

"It's water wonderland, Owen," said Brian. "And it's also deer hunting season."

"Right. So?"

"So, my dad used to hunt. Every year I can remember when he was alive. He had to book his place to stay way in advance. I'm saying, we're screwed. We're never going to get rooms."

Back in the car, Tim pulled out his cell phone and started dialing. For several minutes, the men listened to Tim repeatedly saying, "Nothing available?" He took down numbers on a notepad and called whoever was suggested, but no dice. Finally, he got a bite. "Okay, so you don't have anything? Do you know of— what? What was the name again? Seriously? Um . . . okay. Just a second, I'm writing that down. Okay. Thanks. I will."

"Find something?" Marshall said when Tim hung up.

"Don't know yet. Lemme give this one a call and find out."

Tim dialed and went through his information for what seemed like the twentieth time. Then, his face brightened. "You do? Cabins, you said?" Tim nodded at Marshall, who was watching intently. "How much? Yeah, five guys, right. Yeah . . . um . . . hunting. Right. Just one night. Okay, deal. Lemme give you my credit card number. Really? Okay. Well, thanks." Tim's face had turned a little red. He asked for directions, then hung up, sliding the cell phone back in his pocket.

"Well, guys," he said. "Looks like we're staying at Mustang Sally's."

chapter 30

They decided they'd find the cabins and get settled in as soon as they got to Petoskey. Then, they'd head to Jake's business. It would put them there at about four o'clock, they figured, plenty of time. On the way, they stopped in Indian River to stretch their legs and switch drivers. Brian went into the Mobile Super-Mart and came out with a large bottle of Gatorade. Costa agreed to drive for a while, and Marshall took the front with him. Owen slid into Brian's window seat and leaned his head back and closed his eyes. They were finally off Interstate 75 and heading east on Highway 68 toward Petoskey. It was a winding road, leading them past picturesque farms and rolling hills.

"So, where's this Mustang Ranch, or whatever it's called?" Marshall asked Tim over the seat.

"Mustang Sally's. Out near Pickerel Lake," Tim said, rummaging around. He handed a piece of paper to Marshall. "Directions."

"You're sure we have a place?" said Brian.

"Spoke to Miss Mustang Sally herself," said Tim.

"Mustang Sally," said Costa. "This oughta be good."

"No doubt," said Marshall.

"You didn't give her your card number," Brian said. "You know, to confirm. Don't they all have to do that? Take a credit card number?"

"Yeah," Marshall said. "That's true."

Tim looked down into his lap and fiddled with his cell phone. "Just drop it," he said.

Marshall turned in the seat. "What gives?"

Tim cleared his throat. "She said I sounded . . . real sweet on the phone and that we'd take care of all that business when we got there."

The men burst out laughing. Marshall turned around in his seat and faced the windshield. After a few minutes, softly from the front seat, he began to sing, "Mustang Sally! Hey! Guess you better . . ." he turned and looked at Tim over the seat "slow that mustang down!"

"Fuck you," Tim said, swatting Marshall in the head.

"Say it again," Marshall minced. "You sound so sweet."

Brian and Costa were snickering. Owen snored softly, his head lolling against the window.

Traffic was light. The Navigator rolled down the highway like a big boat on smooth water. Costa drove with one hand on the wheel, his opposite hand draped over the shifter, fingers tapping out a beat to the music playing low on the radio. The men settled in for the last leg of the trip. Marshall gazed out his window, Brian watched the road through the windshield from the back seat, and Tim played a video game on his cell phone.

In the corner, knees up and hands folded between his legs, Owen dreamed. In the dream he was floating on his back on a lake of purple water, staring up at an impossibly blue sky. The waves gently pulled his body out and out, until he realized that he was farther from the shore than he intended to be. A woman stood on the shore. She had her back to him, looking up at the dunes that led down to the water. She had a white wrap around her shoulders, and her long, black hair blew gently in the breeze. Owen wanted to be near the woman. He rolled over on his stomach to swim to the shore, and immediately the sky turned black and the purple water darker, roiling around him, sucking him down. Water sloshed over him, pouring into his lungs. He kicked with all his might, and as his head broke the surface, he could see the woman on the shore had turned toward him and was standing ankle-deep in the water. It was Violet. Above her the sky was still blue and clear, the sun shining down around her, glistening on her glossy black hair. She looked toward him, struggling to stay alive as the churning waters sucked him down again, then buried her face in her hands.

Owen came awake with a start, elbowing Brian hard in the side.

"Ow! Watch it, man," Brian said. "What the hell?"

Owen took a deep breath. "Sorry . . . bad dream. Where are we?"

"Getting close, I think," Brian said. It was late afternoon, and the sun was winking through the trees that lined the winding roadway. Looking out over the hilly landscape, the men could see hints of Lake Michigan in the distance.

Owen shifted in his seat, the residue of the dream sitting like a rock in his stomach. What did it mean? That Violet was sorry? Or that she liked to watch him suffer? Enjoyed the havoc she caused?

"What if we can't find him?" Owen said. "Jake."

"We'll find him," Marshall replied. "We have Internet Genius, here!" He turned and looked at Tim.

"What do you think he's like?" Brian looked crunched in the middle of the back seat between Owen and Tim.

"According to Violet, he's a god among men," Costa laughed.

Tim snorted. "Right."

Owen was like a dog with a bone. "Seriously. What if we can't find him? And if we do, are we going to just barge in on the guy?"

"They barged in on me," Brian said. Costa and Marshall chuckled.

"And what are we going to say to him?"

Tim leaned over and looked at Owen. "Why do you have your underwear in a knot?"

"Shut up," said Owen under his breath, the air getting suddenly tense.

"Can you guys knock it off?" Costa said from the driver's seat. "This traffic is killing me!" Around them now, trucks and campers loaded with hunting equipment were bumper to bumper.

Marshall turned around and leaned over the seat. "Listen, we're almost there. Let's chill, okay? Looks like it's about seven or eight miles to Pickerel Lake."

"At the rate we're moving, that could take an hour," Owen groused.

Marshall sighed and ignored Owen's complaint. He looked at the directions Tim had scribbled on the paper. "And then we have to jog around the lake."

"It is getting late," Brian said, giving Owen a sideways glance. "Are we going to have time to find Jake today?"

"We'll be fine," Marshall said. "What are we looking for?" He turned Tim's crudely drawn map sideways, squinting at it.

"Sally said they were dirt roads," said Tim.

"So, it's Sally now?" Marshall asked, grinning at Tim. Owen sat back and looked out the window, and the mood calmed.

"Shut it," Tim said. He sat up in his seat. "There. Right there. The sign. There's an arrow pointing east."

"What sign?" said Costa, slowing, looking around.

"Mustang Sally's."

"I don't see any sign," Marshall said.

"Right there!" Tim said, pointing out the window as they drove by a small wooden sign set close to the ground. The paint was peeling and it was somewhat askew, as if a car had run into it at some time or other. One corner was broken off, and the vacancy sign hung from one side by a piece of rope.

"Nice," said Owen. "A portent of what's to come."

Tim looked at him and scowled.

"Huh?" said Brian.

"Just saying, if the sign is an indication of what this place is like, I'm sleeping in the car," said Owen.

"Afraid of bugs and crud, are you?" asked Tim.

"Screw you."

Tim laughed. "It'll be fine," he said. "Sally sounded nice on the phone."

"If you recall, Norman Bates sounded nice on the phone, too, when Janet Leigh called to book a room."

"Don't be a pussy, Owen."

Owen made a sudden move toward Tim, shoving Brian back into the seat.

"Hey!" Brian shouted.

"What the hell!" yelled Tim.

"Look—" Owen started, his hands clenching into fists.

They were all thrown forward as the car came to a screeching halt. Costa put the car in park and turned in his seat. "I godda stop the goddamned car like with my kids!?" He looked at the men in the back seat. "Knock it off! Geez!" Tim and Owen sat back sheepishly. Brian shook his head and rolled his eyes. He didn't know what was up between those two, but he sure wished they'd cut it out.

Up front, Costa and Marshall had their heads together over the directions Tim had written. Costa turned off the pavement and onto a dirt road. It was pretty smooth and well taken care of. They drove past a few homesteads, which thinned out after about a mile and a half as pine woods threaded with a few birch, poplar, and the occasional oak. The road narrowed, the trees becoming denser and blocking out the autumn sun. A hawk flew over the road, down low, on the hunt for a mouse or rabbit. Everyone in the back seat was leaning forward as the Navigator humped over the bumps.

"Are you sure that was the right turn?" Tim asked.

"It's what you wrote down," Marshall said. "Then, looks like we're supposed to go to the next dirt road, which is unmarked and only turns off to the left, toward the lake."

"There it is," said Brian, pointing toward a cut in the trees. Costa took the left. The path consisted of two dirt ruts with a hump of grass between. Through the trees, the men could see the intermittent twinkle of water. Owen got a chill, thinking of his dream of drowning in the lake with Violet watching his struggle. He shook it off. What he needed, he thought, was a stiff shot. Maybe they could take care of that once they were settled.

The trees thinned slightly as they approached a medium-sized log cabin set on a little bluff with a horseshoe-shaped dirt drive. It was a bit run down but seemed clean, with three hand-made rocking chairs on the porch and rag rugs. The lake sparkled about two hundred yards behind the cabin, and there was a thin wedge of sand that had most likely been trucked in and poured along the water's edge. Set back in the trees were four or five tiny cabins that looked a little worse for the wear. Owen groaned.

"It don't look so bad," Costa said, opening the door. "Let's go check it out."

"Yeah. Come on." An excitement welled in Marshall, like the one he used to get as a little boy, going to his grandfather's rented cabin on Houghton Lake. He began to stride toward the larger cabin as the others got out and stretched. Marshall saw movement at one of the curtained windows, then the door opened and a woman stepped out on the porch, holding a wooden spoon in her hand.

"You Tim?" she said. The woman had a mass of chestnut hair with a streak of white running through it tied in a loose ponytail with an elastic band. The ponytail hung over her shoulder in a waves that caught the sunbeams, turning her hair to fire. She was wearing men's steel-toed work boots, worn jeans, and a big, soft flannel shirt. Her hands were a little raw, with nails cut short. But it was her face that caught the men's attention: She was quite beautiful in her rustic way, with large green eyes and high cheekbones.

She came down the wooden steps, holding out her hand. "I'm Sally."

"Marshall." He shook her hand. Sally looked at the group. "You're Tim," she said, pointing right to him.

"Yes ma'am," he said, stepping up.

"Enough of that ma'am shit," she said, smiling, her eyes on Tim. "Come on in. I made you some coffee. And we'll take care of business."

chapter 31

The men were divided into two cabins—Costa and Brian in one and the others next door. Though they looked rough on the outside, there were gas heaters inside, log bunks with plenty of warm blankets, and a rough-hewn table in the center of each cabin. There were no bathrooms or running water, but for a few extra bucks Sally had showers outfitted in the basement of her cabin for the campers' use.

Sally didn't take credit cards, so the men had dug through pockets and wallets and come up with most of the cash she required. When she found out Tim was a computer geek, she pulled him aside and told him she'd knock fifty bucks off if he would come in and fix her PC. From the way the two of them had been looking at each other, Marshall suspected she might want him to fix more than her computer.

Owen had been quiet since they'd arrived. He was fiddling with a plastic radio sitting on the windowsill, trying to find a station he could live with.

"Something going on with you?" Marshall asked.

"What do you mean?"

"I don't know, man." Owen had been joking with the other guys, but to Marshall it felt kind of forced.

"What do you care?" Owen snapped. Marshall raised an eyebrow. "Look, I'm sorry, man. I'm kind of keyed up."

"You just don't look too happy about being here, I guess."

"Don't feel one way or the other, I suppose," said Owen. He found a classic rock station on the radio and adjusted the volume, then peered out the window, which was sparkling clean and hung with red checked curtains. The sun dappled the fall foliage and sparkled on Pickerel Lake. "So, what *are* we going to do?" he asked.

"What do you mean? About Jake?"

"Yeah."

"Talk to him, I guess."

"See what he's like, you mean," said Owen.

"Sure."

"Why does it matter?"

Marshall rubbed the shadow of a beard along his jaw. He sighed. "I don't know."

"Violet's going to be pissed," said Owen.

Marshall sat down at the little pine table. "Why do you care so much? I mean, I know you've got feelings for her. I do, too. But don't you want to move on?"

"I don't know," Owen said, turning back to the window.

"You should be more pissed than any of us," Marshall said. "You put up with it longer. Had the most invested when you two split."

"Things happen," Owen said. "Divorce is alive and well in America. Isn't the divorce rate like fifty percent?"

"I don't know." Marshall got a hint of a grin. "With Violet it's at one hundred percent."

"Damn straight. For us, too, when you think about it," Owen said. "Except Costa."

"He's a good guy."

"Yeah."

Marshall looked intently at the other man. "We all are, Owen," he said.

"Yeah." Owen sat up and rubbed at the back of his head. He sighed.

"So, what gives? Why the long face?" Marshall said.

"Maybe I don't want to know what Jake's like. Maybe I don't care," Owen said.

Marshall was quiet for a moment. "Yeah," he said. "I think I know what you mean."

Owen looked at Marshall quizzically. "You don't care either?"

"I don't want to, I suppose," Marshall said. "I guess mostly I don't want Violet to matter."

Owen turned his chair around and scooted it up to the table. "It's okay, you know," he said. "How you feel."

Marshall chuckled, but his eyes were sad. "I'd like to say 'how do you know what I feel like,' but that'd be pretty stupid, now, wouldn't it?"

Owen grinned. "Extremely."

"What is it about her?" Marshall said.

Owen let out a long sigh. "She's Violet. She never knew what she wanted, but for the time she wanted me, I was probably the happiest I ever remember being."

"What about now?"

"I'll live," Owen said.

Marshall gazed out the window. The radio announcer talked about warming temperatures and how it would affect the deer hunting and then launched into Bob Seger's "Night Moves."

"So, why the friendship?" It was the part that confused Marshall the most. He'd been so angry and hurt he couldn't imagine ever being friends with his soon-to-be ex-wife.

"Only way I could be with her," said Owen, fiddling with the zipper on his jacket. "You know how it is. You have to take Violet on her terms or not at all. Anyway, that doesn't matter anymore. I broke things off with her. Friendship-wise."

"Yeah, Tim mentioned that," Marshall said. They were quiet for a moment, then Marshall admitted, "You know, she didn't ask for anything."

"What do you mean?"

"In the divorce papers." Marshall appeared to be studying a silvery scar on the back of his hand. "She didn't want anything from the house. Not even any money. She still has a little left of the trust from Winston. It's in some kind of annuity. Well, you know that, I'm sure."

"Yeah," Owen said. "I set that up for her."

"She didn't want *anything*. Wanted to get it over with fast. No kids, so shit. One day you're married and three weeks later you're not. How does that happen?"

"It happens," said Owen.

"How can you not want anything from . . . from your home?"

Owen recognized the pain in the Marshall's eyes. He pushed his chair away from the table and leaned back and stretched. "You should move."

"Yeah," Marshall said. "I've been thinking about it."

"I'll help you," Owen said.

"Yeah?"

"Sure. I figure I owe you for being such a asshole at first."

Marshall smiled at Owen. "Yeah," he said, "you do."

"So start looking," said Owen. "Shit, you can buy another house. It's a buyer's market."

Tim stuck his head in the door. "You guys hungry?" he asked. "Sally made us some dinner."

"No shit?" Marshall said. "Damn, she really does like you."

"Shut it," Tim said. "It's part of the package. We get dinner and breakfast."

"And maybe more . . ." Marshall laughed.

"Seriously?" Tim raised an eyebrow.

"Hey, we saw how you two were looking at each other," Owen said.

Tim grinned like a schoolboy. "She's pretty, isn't she?"

"Pretty?" Owen said. "Dude, she is fucking gorgeous."

"Seems nice, too," Marshall said.

"She is nice," Tim said. "We've been talking. Oh, and I fixed her computer." He crinkled his brows together. "Satellite Internet. She must pay a fortune for it."

"All the better for cyber chat," Owen said.

"Yeah, yeah," Tim said.

"What about Jake?" Marshall rose from the table and slid his jacket back on.

Tim checked his watch. "Too late to hit him up at work," he said. "Weekend hours. That traffic killed us on time. We're gonna have to figure something else out."

"Well, in that case," Owen said, heading for the door, "let's eat."

PROGRESS NOTES: Violet VanDahmm
     CASE NUMBER: V2011-100982
     DATE: 11-12-2011

SUMMARY:

Violet telephoned the answering service to say she was in an emergency situation. When I returned her call, she was hysterical and crying. She stated she was by the side of the road in a remote location. I asked her if she was in immediate danger, and at this point she explained that she had hit a deer that had run out into the road with her car. She said she was uninjured, but that her car was not starting. She stated that the deer was lying in the road and that some kind of smoke or steam was coming out of her car. I insisted that she hang up and call 911 for assistance. Violet became more agitated and said she was shaking and upset and needed to talk until she was calmer.

At that moment, she told me that the deer was moving. There was a little scream over the line, and then she said that the deer had gotten up and run away into the woods. When she had calmed down, I asked her where she was and told her I could make an emergency call for her from the other line. She stated she was in a town called Indian River and that she was on her way to see Jake

Bowman. I suggested that maybe she could call Jake, and that he could come to assist her, but she stated she could not do that as he did not know that she was coming and that it was a "surprise."

She then told me that a truck with hunters in it had pulled over to help her. I told her to stay on the line with me while she rolled down her window to speak with them. A man agreed to look at her car. She then told me her radiator was broken and that the men offered to drive her a few miles up the road to a place that could fix her car. I told her that it may not be safe for her to do this, but her demeanor had changed from frightened to self-assured. She agreed to call me when she had reached the destination.

Violet called back within twenty minutes. She was upset again, this time because it would take quite a while to fix her car and she would therefore be unable to surprise Jake this evening as she had intended. We discussed whether it was a good idea for her to "surprise" someone she had not seen in more that twenty years. Violet insisted that Jake would "be so happy" to see her. I asked her if she was in a safe place, and she stated the men had dropped her at a diner to await repairs on her car. I told her I looked forward to her next appointment and that we could discuss what transpired at her meeting with Jake. Violet stated, "If things go the way I want them to, I won't need any more therapy!" after which she promptly disconnected.

Yolanda H. Malik, LCSW
Champoor and Associates

chapter 32

Dinner was simple: baked chicken and potatoes with mounds of butter, salad with homemade dressing, and a giant chocolate cake. The men sat around the chunky kitchen table with Sally enjoying their dessert and coffee, rubbing their full stomachs.

"Just what I like to see," Sally said. "Fat, happy men."

"Some of us a little more so than others, eh, Costa?" Tim said.

"Hey," said Costa. "My Angelina got no complaints."

"That your wife?" Sally asked.

"My angel," said Costa. He pulled out his wallet and showed her the photo of his wife and children, and Sally nodded appreciatively.

"What about the rest of you?" she asked. "Married? Girlfriends?"

There was a brief silence. The men looked at each other. "We're . . . um . . . all divorced," Marshall said.

Sally looked around the table, confused at the strange silence. "Hmmmm . . . Okay." She got up and began clearing the dishes.

"Let me help with that," Tim said, and Owen and Marshall snickered. He turned and gave them a black look.

"Oh, honey," Sally said to Tim. "Don't worry about that. You boys are going to want to turn in."

They looked at each other blankly. It wasn't even seven o'clock. Sally shook her head at them.

"Well, breakfast is at four thirty," she said.

Owen's eyes got big. "Four thirty?"

Brian elbowed him, looking at his plate. "Deer hunting," he said down low.

Owen looked as Sally. "We're not hunting," he said, and the other men shot him a look.

"Not hunting?" Sally was confused. She looked at Tim. "What are you doing then?"

Tim looked into Sally's big, green eyes. He liked her. Sitting in her office with her, him at the desk and Sally leaning over him, showing him the problems she'd been having with her computer, Tim felt a warm glow in the pit of his stomach he couldn't remember feeling for a long time. He suspected she was slightly older than him, but it gave her an easiness that younger women didn't have. She wasn't trying to impress him; she was simply being herself.

Her question hung in the air, and Tim couldn't help but answer. He began to tell the story, and as he did, their whole mission sounded idiotic and immature. They'd all been married to the same woman, and now they were going to look up her high school sweetheart before she did, to either warn him or beat the crap out of him. The men squirmed in their chairs. The feeling around the table was very much one of a band of brothers caught doing something naughty by mamma.

Tim sat back down. Sally looked around the table. Then she started to laugh. Not just laughing—belly-clutching, tears-rolling-down-the-cheeks laughing. Uncomfortably, the men started snickering as well, then all-out laughing, looking at each other and pointing, realizing the ridiculousness of the whole thing. Sally sat down beside Tim, getting control of herself. "You mean . . . you mean . . . all of you were . . . married to this Violet?"

Some of the men nodded.

"She must be a hell of a woman!" Sally said, wiping at her eyes.

"She is," said Owen. "She really is."

"Tell me about her," Sally said. "What's she got other women don't?"

"No. No," said Tim. He didn't want to look any more foolish than he already did.

"Come on!" Sally said, laughing. "You have to. Five husbands?"

"Six." Tim said. "Counting—"

"Dead Winston," the rest chimed in.

"Better and better," said Sally. "It's like Liz Taylor." She smacked Tim on the arm. "Inquiring minds want to know." She got a twinkle in her eye. "I know!" she said, popping up and dragging her chair to the sink. She climbed up on the chair and began to rummage in a cupboard, jumping down with a fairly full bottle of Wild Turkey.

"Oh, no," said Owen.

"Oh, yes," said Sally. She twisted off the top and took a sniff. "Yeah, baby." She poured a shot in her coffee cup and passed the bottle to Tim, who did the same. The bottle took a turn around the table.

"To Violet," Sally said. "A hell of a woman." They all toasted and swallowed a shot. "Okay, now. Seriously. All of you married her?"

"Hey, she's beautiful," said Costa.

"And crazy," Marshall added.

"Crazy and beautiful, not always a bad combination," Costa replied.

"What about you, sugar?" Sally said gently to Brian.

Brian shrugged. "I don't know." He looked at Costa. "She was pretty. But she . . . I was always kind of a . . . you know, screw up . . .

because of . . ." his face turned blotchy, "You know, my . . . um . . ." He swallowed the last of his Wild Turkey and looked Sally right in the eye. "I'm bi-polar."

"So?" Sally said, and Brian looked at her gratefully. "Honey, I find normal, whatever that is, kinda scary. Know what I mean?"

"Anyhow, sonny boy," said Costa. "She made you a bundle, huh? In the end?"

Brian gave Costa a warning look. "Shut up!" he hissed.

"Bundle? What are you talking about?" Marshall asked.

"Go ahead. Tell them," said Costa. "What's it gonna hurt, huh?"

"Tell us what?" asked Owen.

"Turns out sonny boy here is a art genius."

"No, I'm not," Brian said, looking down into his lap.

"Come on, sugar," said Sally. "What's the big secret?"

Brian settled back in his chair and took a breath. He told the guys about the offer on the house, the artist retreat, and how the Applewhite the third guy had mistaken him for an artist.

"I don't think it's a mistake," Marshall said when Brian finished.

"What do you mean?" Brian said.

"Well, remember when me and Costa came out there?"

"Like I can forget." Brian smiled.

"I was sitting there looking at that one wall in your living room thinking it was pretty cool. I was even going to ask you to do a wall for me."

"Yeah?"

"No shit," Marshall said.

"Wait a minute," Tim said. "So, this guy is gonna give one hundred thousand for your house? Covered in hubcaps? In Omer? In this economy?"

"I just signed his contract," said Brian.

"Holy shit," said Tim. "Pass me that bottle." The bottle went around the table again, and everyone toasted Brian, whose face was impossibly red.

"It's no big deal," he said. "I didn't even get any money yet."

"No big deal?" said Marshall. "It's a hundred thousand bucks!"

"Yeah, no kidding," said Owen. He chucked Brian on the shoulder. "Congratulations, man."

"Thanks."

"Hey," said Costa. "We godda have you do a wall in the restaurant before you get so famous I can't afford you."

"For you, man, I'll do it for nothing," Brian said. "I owe you."

"Nah," said Costa. "You're a good kid. I want to pay you. You need to value your talent."

"That's right," Marshall agreed.

Sally spoke up. "So, you're doing okay without Violet, hey sugar?" she said to Brian.

He smiled. "I'm better than okay." He looked around the table. "Partly because of these guys."

Marshall winked at Brian across the table. "All I did was make him take a shower," he said.

"Fuck you," said Brian good-naturedly.

The whole table burst out laughing. "He said 'fuck you!'" Tim chortled.

"Shut the fuck up!" Brian said, and there was a new round of laughter.

After the table calmed down, and the bottle went around again, draining it, Sally said, "So, what does this Jake guy have to do with anything?"

All of the guys were curious. Jake Bowman was like a mythical character, made larger than life by the stories Violet told. It was hard not to imagine him as tall, muscular, chiseled, with the well-oiled skin of a romance book cover effigy. You had to hate him on principle. Then again, they'd always carried that same hate for each other, fueled by Violet, to find, upon meeting, they were guys who, outside all that, probably would have sought each other out as friends.

"He was the proverbial 'one that got away,'" Marshall said.

"The one she compared all of us to," Owen added.

"Yeah," said Tim. "I think we just want to know how he did it."

"Did what?" Sally asked.

"Resisted her. Motherfucker must have a will of steel."

chapter 33

Back in their cabin, Costa and Brian sat at the table sipping on honey-sweetened tea Sally sent with them. Brian had a deck of cards spread out on the table playing a game of solitaire while Costa watched.

"You mad at me, sonny boy?" He asked after a while.

"Nah," said Brian.

"I have a big mouth," the Greek said. "Always have. You know how I am."

"I'm learning." Brian flipped over an ace and moved it to the top of his formation, layering a deuce and tray on top. "I've been thinking."

"What about?"

"That artist guy."

"He ain't no artist, sonny boy. He's a art *collector*. There's a difference."

"Yeah. Well. I've been thinking, you know, about when I was doing that."

"What about it?"

Brian set the cards down. He took a drink of his tea. It was soothing and smelled of mint and some other herb Brian couldn't identify. "I wasn't taking my medication," Brian said. "I don't think you can imagine what that's like."

"Like being drunk? Sort of?" Costa suggested.

"No. Not at all," said Brian. He screwed up his face, trying hard to get it right. "You don't know what's real. You know, sometimes I would think I'd said something to Violet or my mom that I didn't say, or think they'd said or done something that didn't happen. Or just didn't remember something that did happen. My head was all screwed up." He took another drink of tea. "And then, see, what happens is, you react like that stuff you imagine is the truth. And it's all messed up."

Costa nodded and just listened. He didn't want to interrupt.

"I'd get so sad," Brian said. "Just so . . . incredibly sad. I'd think, it wasn't worth it, you know?"

"What?" Costa said. "You'd want to kill yourself?"

"I'd be lying if I said I never thought about it." He looked up at the big man and saw that his eyes were misty. "But then I'd get, you know, all this energy. That's the bi-polar thing. You know, you go back and forth."

"Happy and sad?"

"Yeah, but it's like, you know, happy and sad plus. There's no middle."

"So, the pills, they keep you in the middle," Costa said.

"Yeah. Kinda like that."

"So, it's good, right?" asked Costa.

"Well, the thing that's hard is," Brian got a little choked up at this point and Costa politely pretended not to notice. "You miss it."

"How can you miss that, sonny boy? Wanting to kill yourself?"

"Not that," said Brian. "You miss the high. The euphoria, they call it. The meds even you out, but sometimes evened out feels like . . . nothing. Blah." He swallowed. "It's why you keep stopping the meds."

"That what this is about? You want to stop? You stopped?"

"No. No." Brian said. "Shit. This is the best my life has been . . ." He stopped and thought a moment. "I think, ever. I mean since my dad was alive. I was eight when he died."

"What happened?"

"He was drunk. Car accident."

"I'm sorry, sonny boy."

"Thanks." Brian fiddled with the cards. He'd lost interest in the game.

"So, what about the hubcap thing? How'd that start?"

Brian laughed. "Well, I was working out of my dad's old garage. You know, fixing cars. Doing pretty good, too. Of course, Violet hated that. She thought it was stinky and dirty. Put food on the table though."

"Nothing wrong with a man gedding his hands dirty."

"Sure. Well, I was cleaning the garage out one day, you know, because it hadn't really been cleaned out since my dad died and I figured if it was my garage now, you know? So, I'm cleaning it out, and there is this huge bin of hubcaps way in the back under some stuff. Old ones. Like Ford Fairlane wheel covers, and big old chrome Oldsmobile caps. They were cool. And I polished them up, started hanging them on the garage wall. Couple of guys wanted to buy some of them, but I just . . . didn't want to sell them. 'Cause they were my dad's. That's what I told myself anyhow." He tipped back in his chair, teetering on the back legs. "Then one day, it was a Sunday, I think. I was getting pretty trashed." He looked up at Costa. "And yeah, it's a whole different experience getting trashed when you're manic. Anyhow, I get the bright idea I'm going to nail the caps around the front of the house, you know, like a border or something. Violet had been gone about six months, and I guess I finally got it through my thick head she wasn't coming back."

"Yeah," said Costa. "I know how that is."

"So, I take the truck over to the garage and get these hubcaps. I'd started collecting them, too, you know, when I went to the junkyard for parts and stuff, so I had a shitload of them. I take them back to the house and start screwing them to the house. Shoulda seen my mom's face the first time she saw it."

"I'll bet." Costa said. "First time I saw it I thought, what a nut job." Costa swallowed quickly, regretful the moment the words had left his mouth.

"No worries, man," said Brian. "I was a nut job. I just couldn't stop after that. I just kept doing it. Almost fell off the roof one time, putting those sons of bitches up there."

He drained the last of his tea. "'Bout six weeks before you and Marsh came out to my house, I started on the inside. Pretty fucked up, right?"

"Must not be." Costa said. "That Applewhite fella thinks it's art. And you know something? Maybe it is. Maybe you got some, you know, gift."

"Maybe," said Brian. What he didn't tell Costa was how he'd been dreaming about it, about making things out of junk. About how, while they were driving up here, he'd see a hulked-out car or piece of farm machinery rusting in a back yard and think about what he could turn it into with a torch cutter and welder. He thought about the possibilities.

"So, what do you think about going to see this Jake guy?" Costa asked.

"I don't know. I guess I want to see what he looks like, you know? Why do people always care about that?" He fiddled with the deck of cards again. "Used to get so jealous when she talked about him—about you and Winston, too. I thought she did it on purpose to make me mad. Now, I think she just couldn't help it. The way I couldn't help it with the hubcaps."

"I don't know about that," said Costa. "But I know this: Jealousy don't have much to do with love."

"Yeah." Brian tipped his chair forward and leaned on the table. "You think Violet's going to end up with this guy? Owen said she was going to see him."

"I think Violet's good at getting what she wants," said Costa.

"She didn't get what she wanted with him."

"That was then," said Costa. "This is now. Look at us *gáidaros*. Donkeys. We were practice for her."

chapter 34

Tim came in around 11:30 PM. Owen was propped up on his bunk looking at an ancient copy of *Deer Hunter* magazine he'd found in the cabin, and Marshall was sketching something on a newsprint pad he'd brought with him. They both looked up as Tim came through the door, expectant. Tim pulled out his bedding and started making up his bunk while the other two men stared at him.

"What?" he said finally.

"You know what," Marshall said, smirking. "How was your date?"

"That wasn't a date."

"Whaaal," Owen drawled. "Up here in these here backwoods it's a date."

"We just talked."

"Just talked," Marshall said.

"Yeah," said Tim. "She's nice. I think she . . . likes me, too."

"You think?" Owen laughed. "Dude, did you see how she was looking at you?"

"I don't know. She lives way up here, you know?"

"True," said Marshall, turning the pad he was working on, erasing, and drawing in some new lines.

Tim looked at the floor, thinking of his parents. "Plus, my responsibilities at home . . ."

"Right," Owen said.

"Want to hear something fucked up?" said Tim.

Owen leaned on his elbow. "Yeah, man," he said. "We're always in the mood for a fucked-up story."

"Thing is," Tim said, "I haven't even dated anyone since . . . well, there was one girl right after Violet. But that was it. So, it's been like, four years."

"Seriously?" Marshall said.

"Yeah. I was pretty messed up. I worked all the time when I was in Indiana—I mean, *all* the time. Drank some, too. We didn't have any women in my department at work to distract me. I chatted up some online, but that was as close as I got."

"You had cyber sex?" said Owen.

"No, man," said Tim. "Jesus."

"Just asking."

"Well, don't."

Owen shrugged and went back to his magazine.

"So, what's Miss Mustang Sally's story?" Marshall asked Tim.

"Well, this place is hers, forty acres. Used to be a big deer hunter camp. Her husband owned it. I guess there are more cabins further out in the woods—a little more 'rustic' is how Sally described them. Then about twelve years ago, her husband disappeared."

"Disappeared?" Owen swung his legs around and sat on the edge of the bed.

"Yeah," Tim said. "According to Sally there was this big investigation. She even spent some time at the jail. Cops thought she might have offed him. I guess their marriage was less than perfect, and she said everybody knew about it."

"So, what happened to him?" Marshall asked.

"Dunno. I mean, she says she really doesn't know. After eight years she had to have him legally declared dead. She said there were a lot of rumors. Hunters stopped staying here. Gets an occasional group, like us, out-of-towners who haven't heard of her. Says she has a couple families that come every summer. Anyhow, it took her a while to get access to the money—hence the place got run down. She couldn't afford to advertise any more. Just recently got online. That's how I found the place via the Internet on my phone."

"So," said Marshall. "Undead husband, huh? That's some baggage."

"Hey, he's been gone a long time. He has to be dead somewhere, right?"

"Or doesn't want to be found," said Owen.

Tim smoothed his blankets out and gave his bed-making job a cursory glance. He walked over to the table and sat down across from Marshall. "She helped me get Jake's address, though. Some woman she knows uses his landscaping services. She gave her a call and voilà."

"No shit." Marshall yawned. "Cool, man."

"So, what's the plan for tomorrow? I'd kind of like to swing back here on our way back home, tell Sally what happened."

"So," Marshall said, looking up with a half-grin, "You want to see her again."

Tim nodded and scratched his neck nervously. "Yeah. Maybe."

"No maybe about it," said Marsh.

"Okay. I want to see her again."

Owen came over to the table and sat with the other two men. "What *are* we doing tomorrow?" he said.

"Going to check Jake out," said Marshall.

"Should we call him first?" Owen looked from Tim to Marshall.

"Are you kidding?" said Tim. "Would you stick around for that? Hello, Jake? We're a gang of Violet's ex-husbands and we want to pop in and have tea and crumpets. Share our feelings."

"I see your point," said Owen. "So, we're just going to show up."

Marshall shrugged his shoulders. "I guess."

"Not too much enthusiasm there, pal," Owen said. Marshall and Tim sat silent. "We could just go back," Owen continued. "Did anyone think of that?" Owen's head hurt, his conflicting emotions getting the better of him. Why had he agreed to come on this trip? While part of him felt like this was the push he needed to get Violet out of his life forever, for closure, another part didn't want to let her go. A big part. He wanted to get out of here right now, pick up the phone and call her, apologize for cutting her out of his life, get things back to the way they were. To reclaim the possibility of being with her again, even if it was just as friends. But here he was, trapped in a cabin in the woods with all of Violet's exes. He had a feeling things weren't going to end well. "Come on," he said, focusing on Marshall. "Let's just go home."

"I'm tired of going back," Tim said finally. "I want to go forward."

"How Zen of you," Owen said, more snappishly than he meant to.

"You know, you're kind of a pain in the ass," Tim shot back.

Owen clenched his fists in his lap. He was tired from the trip and was not in the mood for any of this guy's shit. He'd been willing to try to like Tim, but wasn't he the one who'd stolen Violet from him in the first place, as easily as he'd stolen that parking space in the lot of Plati Pavlos, without a thought? When Tim married Violet after Owen, he took his place. Owen didn't know if he could ever forgive that. He pushed his chair back and stood up. "You want to settle this, Tim?"

Tim was up and out of his chair. "Let's go, doc," he said.

Marshall stood up. "Knock it off!" he said, looking from Owen to Tim.

Tim leaned toward Owen, pointing a finger in his face. "I didn't trust you from the beginning. I knew there was something off about you. You've been Violet's little bitch—probably running to her, yapping about all of us. How much did you tell her, huh, asshole?"

"Little bitch?" Owen hissed. "You're the pussy that ran away because you couldn't face her!"

Tim stepped forward and grabbed Owen by the collar. He lowered his face to Owen's. "There's a reason you're the one who's always getting punched," he said, smacking him in the jaw. Owen went down like a box of rocks but was up in a flash, punching Tim in his soft middle, doubling him over. Marshall made a grab for Tim, but he shrugged Marshall off easily. Owen made it around to the front of the cabin, where he grabbed a large black umbrella from a stand by the door. It had a long, sharp-looking point on the end, which he stabbed in Tim's direction. When that didn't stop Tim's descent on Owen, he hoisted the umbrella like a baseball bat and brought it down hard on Tim's shoulder, driving him back against the table, which went over with a crash.

Marshall yelled out the door for Costa and Brian, who quickly ran over. Costa pulled Tim away and dragged him into the frigid, dark yard, while Brian and Marshall dispatched Owen, removing his weapon and pushing him down on a log outside. Sally came out on her porch, some thirty yards away. "What the hell you boys doing?" she demanded into the dark. Tim spat at Owen, "You son of a bitch!"

"Prick!"

"Shuddup!" Costa said to both of them. "What the fuck, huh?"

"Don't tell me to shut up, you fat fucking Greek!" Owen yelled.

Costa made it to Owen in two giant steps and had him lofted in the air by his lapels before Brian and Marshall had time to react. Costa stepped forward, pinning Owen to the trunk of a giant pine, knocking the breath out of him.

"You godda big mouth," Costa said.

There was a blast in the air that sounded like a canon going off, and the men whirled toward the cabin, Costa dropping Owen to the ground with a thud. Sally marched over to them holding a rifle.

"Knock it off," she said, quietly. Her soft voice sounded like rain after a symphony of thunder. She was wearing a man's plaid bathrobe over long johns and had the work boots on her feet. Her mass of hair was wild, and her eyes were mean.

"Pack your shit," she said to the men. She reached in the pocket of the robe, extracted a wad of bills, and threw the money down into the muddy leaves. "There's your refund," she said. "I don't need any trouble out here. I've had plenty." She looked at Tim, shaking her head disapprovingly. "Now, get out."

"Sally," Tim said, walking toward her, but she'd already made it to her porch. "I said get out." She didn't look back. There was no doubt in any of their minds that she meant it.

chapter 35

Marshall looked out the diner window. Maude's had been the only place open, aside from a couple of bars that were chock full of deer hunters, and none of the men thought that pouring alcohol on an already flammable situation was a good idea. No Vacancy signs were brightly lit outside the motels, hotels, and cabins along the roadway. It had started to rain a soggy autumn rain, and outside, the smell of molding leaves permeated everything. Marshall had never been happier to get out in the rotten wetness than he was right now. Anything was better than being in the car. The short ride into town from Sally's had been uncomfortable, to say the least, the air inside the Navigator so thick with resentment that it was nearly palpable.

Marshall wiped at the foggy diner window with a napkin and looked across the lot to the car. Owen was hunched down behind the wheel, sulking. Inside the diner, the other four men were sullen, Tim even more so. He sat with his elbows leaning on the table, staring down into a cup of coffee that smelled burnt and acrid.

"Think one of us should go out there?" Marshall said, breaking the silence. Costa and Tim looked up, both giving him a scathing glance. Marshall redirected his gaze to Brian. "You're the only one of us he hasn't gotten into it with."

"And I'm going to keep it that way," Brian answered stubbornly.

Costa and Tim looked pointedly away from Marshall. Everyone was exhausted. To Marshall, it looked like the mission was over. There was nowhere to stay. They were going to have to drive back, which would take four or five hours, depending on the weather, in a car full of pissed-off men. It wasn't a pleasant prospect. He took a deep breath and zipped his jacket.

"Looks like I'm it," said Marshall. No one spoke as he headed out the door into the wet mess. He sighed loudly, his breath fogging out in front of him, and hunched his shoulders up against the cold.

Owen had the heater blasting in the Navigator, and Marshall climbed in to the welcome warmth. For a while neither of them said anything, and they sat watching the drizzle hit the windshield and run down in rivulets. Owen shifted in his seat, stared toward the lights of the diner. "Know why I became a veterinarian?"

"You like animals?"

"No . . . well, yes." Owen turned and looked at Marshall. "But not like some of the others. I mean, I'm good at what I do . . ." He trailed off. Owen wasn't used to talking about himself, to anyone. Not even Violet. But then again, she never really noticed because she was so busy talking about herself.

Marshall waited. He watched a couple of people leave the diner. Tim, Brian, and Costa were the last patrons left. Next to him, Owen sighed.

"I was an only kid. I wanted to be a doctor. A medical doctor, at first." He was staring out the windshield again. "My dad passed away while I was in college. My mom and me—we just never found much to talk about. I made it as far as clinical, and I found out that I just wasn't . . . that good with people."

"You do okay," Marshall said.

"I'm kind of an ass."

Marshall chuckled a little. "Yeah," he said.

"Look," Owen said. "I'm sorry."

"You already apologized to me, man."

"Not for getting us kicked out of Sally's."

Marshall regarded the weather. The rain had picked up. He sure wasn't looking forward to traveling in this. "It is what it is."

In the diner window, the open sign went out. Costa, Tim, and Brian scooted out the diner door, which shut tightly after them, the lights inside immediately going dim.

"Tell him," Marshall said, nodding at the figures approaching the vehicle.

The back door opened, and Brian and Tim slid in.

"Diner closed," Brian said. "They kicked us out."

Costa stood at the driver's door. Owen cracked the door open. "Mind if I drive?" Costa asked him. "I'm too fat for that back seat."

Owen looked over at Marshall, who raised a questioning eyebrow. Owen sighed and slid out of the driver's seat. Costa ducked in, and Owen opened the back door and got in next to Tim, who glanced at him and looked away.

"Hey," Owen said, elbowing Tim gently. He stuck out his hand. "I'm sorry, man."

Tim just shook his head. Owen dropped his hand into his lap and sighed. Marshall peered over the seat at him, nodding toward Tim. "I mean it," Owen said, trying again.

"What's your problem, man?" Tim exploded. "You've been a jerk to me since the first time we met."

"*I've* been a jerk?"

"Son of a bitch!" said Marshall, throwing his hands up in the air.

"What about you?" Owen continued. "You're the one who took her away from me in the first place!"

Silence descended on the men, everyone looking away from everyone else.

"Well," Costa sighed. "As far as that goes, we could just all be mad at each other for that, eh?" He turned in his seat, taking in the others. "Nobody stole nobody. We all know that. Violet just moved on. For whatever reason made sense to her." He looked directly at Owen. "You godda let her go."

"He did." Tim spoke up, and the men turned to him. He looked at Owen. "Didn't you, man?"

"I guess," he said uncertainly.

Tim sighed and looked away for a moment. "Look," he said, turning back to Owen. "I know how you feel. Shit, we all know how you feel." He looked to the other men. Marshall looked away, while Brian nodded solemnly. Costa threw up his hands. Tim reached out and took Owen's hand in his and gave it a rough shake. "We good?" he asked.

"We're good." And then they were quiet, Costa clicking the radio on to static as they pulled out onto the street.

chapter 36

They were crammed in the car in the Kmart parking lot in Petoskey, sleeping. The air reverberated with snoring and was ripe with the morning breath of the five men. They'd tried a few more hotels and motels to no avail. Not only was it deer hunting season, there was some sort of athletic seminar going on as well at North Central Michigan College (go All Stars!), and there wasn't a room to be had for a hundred miles.

Around 5:00 AM, there was a tapping on the window, and Costa came awake with a snort to a policewoman peering in at him and the others. He rolled down the window.

"Sir," she said. "Is there a problem here?"

"No. No, ma'am," said Costa, sitting up in his seat, smoothing his shirt down over his big belly. Next to him, Marshall stirred, as did Owen and Brian in the back of the car.

"Are you men intoxicated?" the officer asked.

"No, ma'am," said Costa. "Got up here last night. No motel."

"Well, it's deer season," said the officer, her voice clearly implying they were idiots.

"Yes, ma'am."

"I'll have to ask you to move along," she said. "No overnight camping is allowed in this lot."

"You got it," said Costa.

"There's a Big Boy up the strip," she said, pointing. "They're open. I expect you'll be wanting some coffee." She walked away shaking her head and said something into a walkie-talkie mounted on her shoulder.

Costa looked at Marshall. "Holy fuck," he said. "I'm gedding old. My back hurts like a son of a bitch."

"I could use a stretch myself." Marshall turned in his seat. "Hey—we have to get out of here."

The cruiser was still parked about one hundred feet away, the officer watching to make sure the men left as she'd instructed.

"I have to piss like a race horse," said Tim, unfolding his body as best he could in the cramped back seat.

"Well, you can't do it here," said Marshall. He looked over at Costa. "Let's roll."

"Well, hit that gas station across the way," said Tim. "Seriously, man, my teeth are floating."

"Mine too," said Brian.

Costa started the Navigator and pulled out of the parking lot under the watchful eye of the officer. They drove slowly up the hilly side street, pulled out onto Mitchell, Petoskey's main artery, and crossed to the gas station. Everyone chipped in, and Owen gassed up the car while each of them took a turn in the rest room.

Half an hour later they were sitting in the Big Boy, plates of pancakes, scrambled eggs, and bacon before them, as well as steaming cups of coffee. Tim was mopping up syrup from his plate with a piece of toast.

"So, what you're saying," he said to Marshall, "is that none of us knows what Jake looks like."

"I've seen yearbook pictures," said Owen.

"But you know how that is. Hell, when I was seventeen I had great hair, a six pack, and no glasses," continued Marshall.

"Shit," said Costa. "I still look good."

"Yeah, you're a goddamned Adonis," said Owen.

"Good of you to notice." Costa slid two slices of bacon between two pieces of toast and bit into it.

Owen nudged Costa. "We're all pretty swanky guys, eh?"

Costa nodded.

"Look," Owen said, addressing the table. "I just want to say—"

"Forget about it," Costa interrupted.

"No, I—"

Costa set his toast down on his plate. He looked at Owen. "You really sorry?"

Owen looked sincere. "Yeah."

There was a moment of silence, then Costa said, "Good, then you can pay for breakfast!" The whole table laughed. The waitress came and poured them all another round of coffee.

"So, we're going to go to Jake's house," Owen said, "then what?"

"We tell him Violet's through with us and now it's going to be his turn in the hot seat. I think he should know a few things prior, is all I'm saying," Tim said.

Brian had been fairly quiet throughout breakfast, but now he spoke up.

"He's probably married," he said. The table went quiet.

"Yeah," Marshall said. "What if he's married? Has a family?"

"Not really any point to this, then, is there?" Owen said.

There was a moment of silence as the men looked at each other. Then Brian said, "Owen has a point."

"True," Costa said. "But aren't you just a little curious about this *bástardos* Violet was always comparing us to?"

"Yeah, man," Tim said. "As Miz Mustang Sally says, inquiring minds want to know."

Marshall looked around the table. "But, you know, if you think about it, aren't we all better off? I mean, right now. Just take Jake out of the equation for a minute. Aren't we better off than we were before we met?"

"I don't know, crazy ass," said Costa laughing. "You busted up my restaurant."

"You know what I mean, man."

"Of course I do, sonny boy. We're like brothers. Eat together, drink together, talk. We even fight together like brothers."

"But aren't any of you still pissed off?" Tim said. "About what she did to you? What she did to all of us?"

"Hell, yes," said Marshall. "I'm still pissed. It's only been a couple months since we split up. But, the divorce is already final, zipped up. So what good does being pissed off do me?"

"Let's just get a look at the guy," Tim said. "Then, if you guys want to go home, we'll go home. I mean, we came a long way . . ."

"A look. So, what are we going to do?" Owen said. "Park across the street and spy on him? Jesus. Isn't that a little too tenth grade?"

"Yes. And fuck you," said Tim. He gave Owen a nod. "Okay. You have a point."

"Can't we just tell the truth?" Brian said.

The table went silent.

"You mean, just walk up and ring the bell and say we're Violet's ex-husbands?"

"Well, aren't we?" Brian said.

chapter 37

It was a nice house, built of log with large windows and a red metal roof. The front yard was landscaped with shrubs and autumn flowers: brightly colored chrysanthemums, fire bushes turning glowing red, and bluish junipers loaded with berries. There was a stone path leading from the driveway to the front door, which was painted white and decked out with a brass knocker. The rear of the house butted the water, which the men could see sparkling beyond the garage and back yard.

"What did I tell you?" Brian said, gazing at the nicely kept house and lawn. "Definitely a woman lives here. Look at those little angel statues in the flower bed."

"I'm with Brian," said Owen. "What if his wife is home by herself, huh? All of us showing up at the door will freak her out."

"Guys can't have nice houses?" Marshall said, and Tim nodded in agreement. "He owns a landscaping business—of course his yard looks great."

They sat parked across the road, staring at the house, each lost in their own thoughts for a moment. Tim broke the silence. "Maybe he's gay," he said.

"What?" said Owen. "Nah."

"Maybe he is," Tim insisted.

"I don't know . . ." Brian said uncertainly.

"Let's just check the situation out," said Costa. "Geddit over with, huh? I promised Angelina I'd get back in time to do something with her and the kids tonight."

"Let's just get out of here," Owen said. "This is stupid. And Violet's gonna be—"

"Who gives a fuck how she feels?" Marshall snapped. "Enough already!"

"Yeah, man," said Tim. "I say we go in."

Costa threw up his hands. "Jesus Christ! What the hell are we doing?"

The car door popped open and Brian stepped out on the sidewalk. "I'll go." The other men's mouths dropped open in surprise. Brian closed the door, and Marshall reached over and powered the window down.

"What are you going to say?" Marsh asked.

"I dunno," said Brian. "If his wife—or whoever—answers, I guess that we're friends or something?"

"Don't freak her—or whoever—out," Tim said.

Brian started away from the car. "I won't. Not any more than any of you freaks would anyhow."

"Kid's godda point." Costa shrugged.

Marshall closed the window as the men sat watching Brian walk up the little stone path with his hands shoved in the pockets of his jacket. He stood for a moment on the stoop, then rang the door bell. After a few moments, a man opened the door.

Tim reached over and gave Owen a sock on the arm. "Get a load of him." Costa gave a low whistle. "Holy shit. That son of a bitch looks good."

Marshall leaned forward, squinting. "Maybe it's not him."

They all stared while Brian continued to talk to the man on the stoop. Owen self-consciously sucked in his gut. The guy at the door was fit, tanned, and had a shock of blond hair that swept over his forehead. Owen reached up and worried at his own thinning dome. No wonder Violet couldn't forget the guy. He looked like a movie star.

The man shook hands with Brian, who gestured toward the car. They looked toward the Navigator and waved. Costa, Marshall, Tim, and Owen waved back weakly.

"What the hell's he doing?" said Tim. Brian was gesturing, waving to them to come out.

"Shit," said Owen. "Now what?"

"Ged outta the car, dumb ass." Costa climbed out onto the pavement. Brian and the man were walking toward the car.

"Hey, guys," said the man.

"Hey," said Marshall, going forward and extending a hand. "Marshall VanDahmm."

"Paul Spiker."

"Paul lives here with Jake," said Brian.

"We've got the right house then," Tim said.

"Sure," Paul said. "Jake's not here right now, though. I was just telling Brian. He had some sort of meeting in town. You guys drive a long way?"

"Saginaw area," said Tim.

"Wow," said Paul. "That is a drive. Brian said you guys are friends of Jake's? He didn't say anything about you coming."

"It's kind of . . . a surprise," said Marshall.

The men shifted uncomfortably. "I know he's from that area," continued Paul. "Why don't you come in? I can give Jake a call on his cell and see how long he's going to be."

"Um . . . no," said Owen.

"Sure," said Marshall.

"I don't know," said Brian.

"Yeah," Tim said, and Costa shrugged.

Paul looked at them quizzically. "Sounds to me like you guys need a beer." He chuckled. "Come on in. I have some cold ones in the fridge. You can walk out and take a look at the water while I call Jake and let him know you're here."

"That'd be cool, man," Marshall said, throwing Owen a look that said shut up. Owen looked the other way and shoved his hands in his pockets.

"So strange that Jake didn't say anything about friends coming up," said Paul.

"It was one of those, you know, spur-of-the moment things," Tim said. "You know, having a few drinks, talking about old times. We just decided to surprise him."

"No shit?" said Paul, holding the door open for them.

"No shit," said Costa.

Paul led them through the interior of the immaculate home. The rear wall of the house was glass and looked out at the water, where the sun sparkled, making thousands of tiny diamonds dance on the surface.

"Great place," Marshall said.

"Thanks," said Paul. "As soon as it listed, I put an offer on it. I'm in real estate." He opened a little wooden box on the counter and pulled out a stack of business cards, handing one to each of the men. "Case you're ever in the market for property up here in the Great White North."

Beers in hand, Paul led them out a back sliding glass door to a deck that extended out to the water. Paul leaned on the rail. "Definitely the life," he said. He smiled at them, flashing his white teeth. The sun shown off his tanned, muscular lines, and the men couldn't help but wonder if Jake looked as good as this guy. In the quiet, they suddenly heard the sound of a car turning in the drive.

"Well, there he is now." Through the screened windows they could hear the sound of the front door opening. "Out here!" Paul called.

All of the men were holding their breath, waiting to get a look at the guy who'd had the ability to hold Violet's attention for more than twenty years. The man who stepped out onto the deck was as regular as each of them, slightly graying at the temples of brush cut hair, a little soft in the belly, wearing shorts, a button-down shirt, and a pair of well-worn loafers. There was nothing remarkable about him, save for his bright green eyes what were crinkled at the corners with laugh lines.

Looking as radiant as ever stood Violet, holding Jake's hand. It's hard to say whose eyes went wider in surprise: Jake's at seeing a deck full of strangers, the men at seeing Violet, or Violet herself at being confronted with an army of her past. She dropped Jake's hand, unsure of what was going on, whether he'd led her into some sort of trap. She looked panicked, at the faces of each of her ex-husbands, a keening sound coming from the back of her throat. The exes stood stock-still as statues, tongues tied.

Jake and Paul looked at each other, confused. "What the hell's going on?" Jake said.

Violet fainted dead away onto the deck.

For a moment no one moved. The men looked at each other, each taking a hesitant step toward Violet, then stopping, ogling each other. Paul looked around, exasperated. He set his beer down on the deck rail. "I've got her," he said, swooping Violet up in his beefy arms and carrying her inside.

"Who the hell are you people?" Jake asked, his face a mask of confusion.

"A bunch of fucking morons," said Owen. "That's who." He broke away from the group and followed Paul inside.

chapter 38

"Well, that's par for the course," said Tim, watching Owen go.

"Don't bust the guy's balls," Marshall said. "He's just . . . worried about her."

"Who are you again?" Jake asked. A sheen of sweat had broken out on his forehead. He looked from one guy to the next.

Marshall stepped up. "Sorry, man," he said, extending his hand. "Marshall VanDhamm."

Jake tentatively stuck out his hand. "Violet's . . . ex-husband?"

"Yeah," Marshall said.

Jake put both hands up. "Look," he said, "I don't want any trouble—"

"No trouble," said Tim, stepping in and shaking Jake's hand. "Tim Stark. I'm . . . I'm an ex, too."

"Brian Jankowicz."

"Me. I'm Costa."

Jake stood looking at the four of them, dazed. He aimed a thumb toward the house. "I assume he's an ex, too?"

"Yeah," said Marshall. "That's Owen."

"What the hell are you doing here?" Jake sputtered.

The men looked sheepish. Caught in the midst of a situation they created, they had no idea what to say.

"We thought we'd get here before her," said Tim.

"Wait a minute," Jake said. "You guys knew she was coming here?"

"Owen knew," said Marshall. "She told him she was coming to look you up. The 'one that got away,' in Violet's words."

Jake looked thoughtful. "About that—" he began.

"Jesus, you're all she ever talked about," said Tim.

"And talked and talked and talked." Costa swallowed the remainder of his beer. "Jake this. Jake that."

"So, what did you intend to do?" Jake asked.

Marshall, Tim, Costa, and Brian looked at each other. Costa shrugged. "We got no fucking idea," he said.

Brian spoke up. "We just wanted to . . . see . . . what you were like."

"See what I was like?"

"Yeah, dude," Tim said. "You're like . . . a superstar." He looked around at the other guys. They were nodding.

"Excuse me?"

"Well, we wondered how you'd been able to say no to Violet," Marshall said. "And, I mean . . . I guess . . ." his face turned red, "I guess we get that part now."

Jake's face flushed slightly. "O . . . kay," he said slowly.

"We thought you were, like, some kind of romance hero," said Tim.

"Yeah," said Costa. "And look at you. I mean, you look just like—"

"Us," Tim and Marshall finished.

"Yeah," Costa said. "Just like us *ilíthioi.*"

"What'd he say?" asked Jake.

"He said we're idiots," Brian answered.

"So," Tim said, grinning. "We have to know . . . I mean, Violet must have been a stone fox in high school."

"She was something," Jake said. He broke out in a smile.

Behind Jake the sliding glass door slid open, and an irate Paul stepped out on the deck. "Do you know who these guys are?" he demanded. "They told me they were friends of yours."

"Yes," said Jake, sighing.

"Yes, you know who they are or yes, they're friends."

Jake looked uncomfortable. "I think . . . both," he said to Paul.

Paul sighed. "Well, we have a hysterical woman sobbing all over our Eames sofa. What are these *friends* of yours going to do about that?"

Jake clenched his jaw. "Look, just stop it," he said. He put his hand on Paul's arm. "Is she okay in there?"

"Yeah," said Paul, keeping his eyes on the other men. "That Owen guy is fawning all over her."

Tim rolled his eyes.

"Would you see if Violet or Owen need anything?" Jake said. "I want to talk to these guys for a minute."

"Sure." Paul said. He gave the men a confused look and headed back into the house.

Jake looked at the others. "Let's take a walk down to the water," he said.

chapter 39

In high school, Violet was one of those girls boys dreamed about but seldom dated. She wasn't "in style," didn't go to the usual hangouts, and she was constantly reading, her smoky eyes behind a pair of funky glasses. The reading gave the impression of intelligence, though in reality, Violet was an average student, prone to daydreaming.

She had a body, but it wasn't the tall, thin Barbie doll body that was the ideal. She was round and curvy and soft. She had a great laugh. She'd touched you on the arm, the shoulder, and she wasn't afraid to talk to the boys, nor did she play the flirty games the popular girls did, ignoring you when they really wanted your attention because they knew it would drive you crazy. If Violet wanted you, she just said so. Or did something that made you know.

With Jake it happened in art class, like Violet had told each of them, but according to Jake it was Violet who'd reached under the table that day, grabbed his hand and placed it on her leg. He'd liked it, or thought he did. More accurately, he wasn't really sure what he liked. He'd been living too long in a household filled with his parents' loveless marriage. It was hard to know what a real relationship was supposed to be like. All he remembered were periods of bitter arguing and silence. Clocks ticking and uncomfortable dinners, he and his siblings swinging their legs under the table while his parents avoided eye contact and made a big deal of chewing and swallowing their food, getting meals over as quickly as possible.

He still remembered the way her skin felt. She'd been wearing a short skirt and knee socks. She was softer than anything he ever remembered touching, and the heat of her made him tingle from head to toe. She sat so still, barely breathing, letting him touch her leg, hold her hand. It was what he was supposed to do, right? He was in high school. He was supposed to feel up girls whenever he had the chance, right?

But more than excitement, he was curious. The feel of her elicited something other than a sexual response, more of a curiosity over the intimacy of it. Home was so bereft of anything warm and intimate, and this felt so tender. He would have liked to hug Violet, but he knew she wanted something more from him. Something he was not sure he could give her.

He didn't want to mess anything up though, just in case. Just in case he really didn't like boys. He thought he might, and he still felt . . . unnatural about it, and scared, too. He had no one to talk to. How do you tell other guys you might be queer? How do you tell anyone? Back in the 1980s you didn't talk about it, not in a small town in Michigan anyhow. Not in their school. And what if he wasn't? Violet liked him. Jake liked her, too. She was pretty and smart and funny. She'd make a good girlfriend. Just in case.

So, they'd hung with the same crowd, did lots of things together, but never dated. At first, Violet just thought he was shy, then later, after his parents divorced, he was so broken up over it that he couldn't face having a relationship. She wrote him long letters, telling him how much she cared about him, that she understood, that she'd wait for him. Sometimes he felt bad that he was dishonest with her, especially when he started experimenting with other guys and he was pretty sure about his orientation. But he kept hearing how teens go through phases, and they grow out of behaviors, and what if it was a phase?

After high school, he couldn't bring himself to tell her. He almost did once, and she'd dissolved into tears believing he was in love with another girl. No matter how many times he told her that wasn't it, she kept saying how she'd seen the signs, and how could he? She'd been there for him all this time. What was wrong with her? Wasn't she attractive?

After that, Jake enrolled in the service. After nearly a year, he started writing to her. They'd kept in touch until she married Winston. He'd gotten a few letters from her after that, then the occasional Christmas or birthday card, and then they'd lost touch altogether. Then, some twenty years later, she finds him here in Petoskey. It had been a shock.

The men were on the little stretch of beach at the rear of the house, sitting in cloth chairs, looking out at the water.

"So, she knows now," said Marshall, looking out over the lake. Tim and Costa stood side by side in the sand, listening, and Brian was sitting cross-legged on the ground.

"Yes," Jake said. "That's why I brought her back here. To meet Paul. We've been together for six years now."

"That's great, man," Tim said. "Having someone in your life."

"Yes," said Jake. "It is." He grinned. "Even though he's a little . . . overprotective sometimes."

"How'd she take it?" Marshall asked.

Jake sighed. "It was hard." He looked out at the sun glinting on the water. His eyes were a little misty. "She cried a lot. Wanted to know why I'd never trusted her with it."

"You shoulda told her," Costa said. "Would have been better for everyone. Including all a us."

"No kidding, man," Tim said. "Between you and Dead Winston, us schmucks didn't stand a chance." He chuckled.

"Sorry about that," Jake said. "I really am."

"She always thought something was wrong with her," Brian said. "She'd get all sad about it."

"I know I hurt her," Jake said. "I feel horrible. If it's any consolation, for anyone, we're going to make a new stab at being friends—real friends this time."

"That's good," Brian said.

"It is," Jake replied. "So, you guys showing up on top of my news . . ."

Tim grinned. "Yeah," he said. "She's probably really freaked out."

"No doubt," said Brian.

"So, now what?" Jake looked at each of the men.

"No fucking clue," said Marshall.

The sliding glass door opened, and Paul stepped out onto the deck just as the sound of tires spinning in gravel issued from the front of the house. All the men looked toward the street to see Violet's Volvo, Owen in the driver's seat, pulling hurriedly away.

"Where the hell are they going?" said Costa.

Paul was walking toward them. "I heard the guy say something about some hotel. She said she couldn't face all of you again." He held the keys to Owen's Navigator out to Marshall and dropped them in his palm. Marshall stood with his mouth hanging open and watched dust rise behind the retreating Volvo.

"Holy shit," he said.

PROGRESS NOTES: Violet VanDahmm
    CASE NUMBER: V2011-100982
    DATE: 11-17-2011

SUMMARY:

Violet called prior to the appointment to say that she wished to bring her ex-husband, Owen, along for a joint session. With some hesitation I agreed, but I explained I would like to speak with Violet for a few minutes prior to speaking to the couple together.

Violet shared her embarrassment regarding the trip to Petoskey and for the first time exhibited a bit of insight into her own psyche, saying "I'm afraid I have a bad habit of leaping before I look." She told me that she had a lot to talk about regarding the weekend, but that today her main consideration was Owen, who'd followed her north and "rescued" her.

Violet stated that she was "angry at" herself for how she has treated "someone who cared for me no matter what," and how she refused to see this because of her own "selfishness." I told Violet how proud I was of her for this bit of self-examination, and we talked about ways to learn from this rather than delving into self-deprecation.

We then invited Owen into the session. He seemed very uncomfortable, but he sat next to Violet on the sofa and took her hand, a very tender gesture. I asked the couple what brought them in to therapy together today. Both were silent for a moment, and I admit I expected Violet to dominate and take over the session, but she demurred, looking to Owen.

Owen shared that the two of them had driven to Traverse City and taken some time to really talk about the past and about the friendship they'd shared after their divorce. He stated that at one point, the conversation had gotten so heated that the hotel manager had come to the door to see if there was a problem and to warn them to be quiet. After the manager left, Owen said he'd shut the door and he and Violet had looked at one another and started laughing.

The couple looked at one another then, and I could see them smiling, as if they would revisit the mirth they'd experienced in the hotel room.

Violet shared that they hadn't been able to stop laughing—and that that laughter had segued into tears of sadness for her. She said Owen had held her then, and she realized in that moment how much he cared for her and what a gift that was.

They were both silent again, and so I asked them how I could help them. Owen looked to Violet. They still had their hands clasped, and she nodded at him. He turned to me and said that they wished to attend therapy together with a goal of possible reconciliation. I explained to the couple that with so much water under the bridge, old hurts, other relationships, that this would be a lot of work.

Owen looked tenderly at Violet and said, "Oh, boy, do we know that."

I recommended some private sessions for Owen, and therapy as a couple to continue twice per month, unless otherwise indicated.

Violet handed me her journal then and asked that I read it after they'd left. Upon opening it, there was a single line written on the first page. It said, "Thank you."

Yolanda H. Malik, LCSW
Champoor and Associates

chapter 40

Outside, snow was falling. Marshall climbed down from the ladder and stood with his hands on his hips and looked out the huge picture window at the stuff collecting like fairy dust on the shrubs and pines. He was glad he'd gotten the yard cleaned up and bushes trimmed before this first good snowfall. He owed Tim his thanks for that. He'd come over and spent a whole Saturday mowing and clipping and bagging up yard waste right alongside Marshall. He'd been the first one to come and help him work on the house.

He turned and surveyed the mess on the inside. Today he'd been sanding the new crown molding, and there was plaster dust all over the place. The floor was bereft of carpeting, and Marshall was planning on sanding and finishing the wood that had been revealed beneath. There were splotches of plaster drying on some of the old existing walls where he'd had to make repairs. He rubbed at his head and smiled when plaster dust fell away from him in a cloud. Everything was a mess, but he was the happiest he'd ever been.

He stood, looking around at the new configuration of space, and was pleased with the layout he'd devised with the help of the contracting firm's designer. In addition to being talented, she was attractive, in a quiet, intelligent way that Marshall found intriguing. He'd thought about asking her out, and he sensed some interest on her part as well, but he just didn't have his land legs back quite yet. *Soon, though,* he thought, *soon.*

From out back, where the property butted up to a few acres of woods, a series of barks issued, startling Marshall from his reverie. He'd adopted three young Boston terriers he'd named Larry, Moe, and Curly, and they were letting him know it was time to come back in. He smiled to himself. He had to admit, the remodel and all the hard work that came with it had been just the thing he'd needed.

So far, he and the guys had finished his bedroom and a bathroom, and they had gotten the kitchen back into usable shape. Now he spent his weekends—and several evenings—lovingly sanding and painting and constructing. He liked seeing tangible proof of the progress he was making as he worked at the remodel. He felt energized, even at work, and had been sleeping better. He knew the friendships he'd forged were part of it. Regardless of the rocky starts they'd all had, they were part of something. It had been shaky with Owen after Petoskey, but the group was slowly somehow coming around to the idea of Owen and Violet together.

At first, watching Owen drive away in Violet's Volvo that chilly Sunday afternoon had felt like a betrayal. Tim, of course, had been the most vocal, with Marshall not far behind. Brian, as usual, was introspective as Costa drove Owen's car south, his eyes on the road, not saying much. Later though, it was Costa who'd put in into perspective. "Love's love," he'd said. "You think you got control, but it picks you." Owen couldn't help it, Marshall knew that now. He loved Violet. No matter what he'd gone through with her, or the rough time the guys had given him about her, Owen had remained steadfast. And to her credit, it seemed like Violet was trying hard to make things work this time around.

A little part of that niggled at Marshall, of course: *Why the effort to work it out with him and not me?* Marshall was pretty sure that all the guys had thought the same thing, at least for a minute. But hadn't things worked out better for all of them? In the course of the divorce, what Marshall had realized was that he truly was better off. The renewed spirit that refurbishing this old house gave him had confirmed that. Costa was right. Love's love. It was bigger than any of them.

Marshall let the dogs in and gave them all a treat, the three of them sitting before him like a chorus line, wiggling their butts. Owen had hooked him up, making sure the puppies were healthy, advising Marshall on the breed's characteristics and inclinations. Marshall'd loved them from the start. They were playful and sweet, and Marshall had needed to feel needed.

When he had gotten home that night from the Jake escapade, Marshall'd stood on the sidewalk looking at the house. The simple split-level was nice, but it had never really grabbed him. It was in a nice neighborhood, close to downtown, had good bones, good landscaping. And Violet had liked it. That had been all he cared about at the time. He had talked to Owen about it being a buyers' market and the possibility of getting a different place, but suddenly he found himself with a mission.

Marshall strode through the house, turning on lights in every room, searching for something, some sense of home, some feeling that tied him here, but there was nothing. Even the comforting nest he'd created for himself in the living room made him feel nothing more than sadness for the part of him that had spent numerous sleepless nights here. Yes, he'd thought, he could sell it. Or . . .

In the kitchen, he'd put water on for tea and fired up his laptop at the table, suddenly excited. As he'd waited for water to boil, he'd punched *Saginaw Bay Area residential contractors* into the search engine and watched as several businesses with building and remodeling experience populated the screen, lighting his eyes.

That had been only eight short weeks ago. He'd jumped on the remodel hungrily, working hand in hand with the contractor and the designer, Marianna. He smiled thinking of her, her shocking red hair, her blue eyes encased by severe, mannish glasses. Around him, magic had happened. A place to live had finally turned into a home.

Outside, a car horn honked furiously. Marshall left the pups chewing on their treats and walked into the living room, glancing out the picture window. Owen's SUV was pulling into the driveway. He waved through the window as the gang of guys popped doors open and slid out of the vehicle, all wearing their old jeans and sweatshirts. True to form, Costa walked around back and hauled out a large cooler, and Tim was carrying a brown bag, no doubt filled with cold beers. Costa and Tim began walking toward the front door. Marshall opened it for them as they tromped up the front steps and knocked the snow off their shoes.

"Gimme a hand," Costa said, grunting, and Marshall reached out and took the cooler from him.

"Come on in," he said. "What are Owen and Brian doing out there?"

"Check it," said Tim, inclining his head toward the front door. Owen came through backward carrying one end of a large box. Brian was on the other end.

"What the hell?" said Marshall.

"Big-screen TV," said Costa. "It's Sunday. We're watching the game."

Marshall broke out into a huge grin. "Are you guys kidding me?"

"Nope," Owen said, he and Brian setting the box down on the living room floor. "It's from all of us."

"But—I don't even have the cable hooked up," Marshall said weakly.

Tim grinned. "Yes, you do."

Brian shut the door. "Let's set this up," he said. "I'm starved."

Marshall looked at the assembly of men standing in his home. "You guys are too much."

"Nah," said Costa, waving a dismissive hand. "We're just enough."

Marshall patted his former nemesis on the back and grinned. "Yeah," he said. "You've got that right."

In the kitchen, Marshall opened the pantry door. It was one of the only spaces that had been left untouched by the remodel, and as such, bore the brunt of it. Boxes of packed items were stacked on the shelves and the floor. Today felt like a celebration, and Marshall was sure there were some nice beer glasses on one of the shelves—glasses Violet had gotten him in Frankenmuth when they were still together. He got lucky with the second cupboard. Sure enough, tucked close to the back was a box from Alpine Outlet containing the glasses.

Marshall pulled it toward him, dust shifting down from the shelf. He climbed down, the box in his hands, and took it in to the kitchen, setting it on the new marble counter. He popped the top of the box open. Lying there on top of the beer glasses were three photographs, the first two of Violet and him hoisting mugs of ale at the Frankenmuth World of Beer Festival. He remembered they'd put the photos in there as a reminder of the beautiful day they'd had. It was the spring before they'd gotten married, and they looked deliriously happy and a good bit drunk. The third photo had been taken at sunset, with Violet standing in profile on the covered wooden bridge. The breeze blew her hair gently away from her porcelain features. She was looking off into the distance, as if she could see what awaited her there, a half smile on her face. Marshall remembered how his heart had caught in his throat, watching her standing there, so he snapped this picture.

He smiled softly, then tossed the photographs into the waste basket. It wasn't some deep gesture of how he'd parted ways, but rather just a practical, natural action like rinsing and drying the glasses he took from the box one by one.

In the living room, the men poured beer, and Tim took a break from busily hooking up the big-screen television. Costa, ever the life of the party, hoisted his glass. "To sonny boy," he said, smirking at Marshall, "and his beautiful, messed-up house!"

"Cheers!" Brian said, and the men clinked glasses and drank deeply.

"Now, hurry it up," Costa said to Tim. "The game's on in twenty minutes."

"You are one bossy son of a bitch," Tim said, grinning.

"Come on," Brian told him. "I'll help you."

Costa headed into the kitchen to put some food in the oven to heat, and Tim and Brian got busy hooking up cables and wires. Marshall walked over to Owen, who was standing at the window, watching the snow fall softly on the world outside. "Hey," Marshall said, nudging him.

"Hey." Owen turned to him. "Congratulations on the house, man. It's really coming together."

"Thanks." Marshall thought about the photograph of Violet on the bridge. He chucked Owen on the arm. "You're a lucky guy. I really wish you and Violet the best of luck."

"Thanks," Owen said. "That means a lot." He took a long drink of beer and stared out across the front lawn, a faraway look on his face. "We'll see what happens, I guess."

Marshall wasn't sure what to say. He thought about the chance Owen was taking. It was bigger than his tearing out walls and windows, and even, possibly, dating someone new. Owen was taking a chance with his life and his heart with his eyes wide open. The two men stood beside each other, looking out at the falling snow.

Behind him, Marshall could hear the sounds of Tim swearing and Brian cajoling, Costa in the kitchen banging against pans, and Larry, Moe, and Curly playing together on the rug. He'd never felt more at home in this house, even though there were beams exposed and walls unfinished and shedding plaster dust. "I guess," he said finally, "It's having the guts to try. To start over." He raised his glass. "You've got guts, man."

Owen grinned. "Don't we all." He raised his glass to meet Marshall's. "Here's to guts!"

acknowledgments

I would like to thank Jeff VandeZande for mentoring and encouraging me these past few years. You are more friend than teacher, and for that I am grateful. Thank you for validating my efforts and my continuous "return to the fire."

I would like to thank the Skip Renker Foundation, the League for Innovation Awards committees and the Fabri Literary Prize committee for your belief in my work. I also have a special place in my heart for Bob Dourandish at pixelhose.com who continues to support and market my writing. Thank you to a great editor, Roxy Aliaga, and to the team at Counterpoint for making the publishing process as painless as possible.

Finally, thanks to Omar O. Nelson for patiently, silently overseeing the writing and editing process. You're a good cat.